STORIES
FOR THE YOUNG

BY

HANNAH MORE

For The Young Stories

BLACK GILES THE POACHER

This story exhibits an accurate picture of that part of the country where the author then resided; and where, by her benevolent zeal, a great reformation was effected among the poor inhabitants of at least twenty parishes, within a circle of thirty miles.

Poaching Giles lives on the borders of one of those great moors in Somersetshire. Giles, to be sure, has been a sad fellow in his time; and it is none of his fault if his whole family do not end their career either at the gallows, or at Botany Bay. He lives at that mud cottage, with the broken windows stuffed with dirty rags, just beyond the gate which divides the upper from the lower moor. You may know the house at a good distance by the ragged tiles on the roof, and the loose stones which are ready to drop out from the chimney; though a short ladder, a hod of mortar, and half an hour's leisure time would have prevented all this, and made the little dwelling tight enough. But as Giles had never learned any thing that was good, so he did not know the value of such useful sayings as, that "a tile in time saves nine."

Besides this, Giles fell into that common mistake, that a beggarly looking cottage, and filthy, ragged children, raised most compassion, and of course drew most charity. But as cunning as he was in other things, he was out in his reckoning here; for it is neatness, housewifery, and a decent appearance, which draws the kindness of the rich and charitable, while they turn away disgusted with filth and laziness: not out of pride, but because they see that it is next to impossible to mend the condition of those who degrade themselves by dirt and sloth; and few people care to help those who will not help themselves.

The common on which Giles' hovel stands is quite a deep marsh in a wet winter, but in summer it looks green and pretty enough. To be sure, it would be rather convenient, when one passes that way in a carriage, if one of the children would run out and open the gate; but instead of any one of them running out as soon as they hear the wheels, which would be quite time enough, what does Giles do but set all his ragged brats, with dirty faces, matted locks, and naked feet and legs, to lie all day upon a sandbank hard by the gate, waiting for the slender chance of what may be picked up from travellers. At the sound of a carriage, a whole covey of these little scarecrows start up, rush to the gate, and all at once thrust out their hats and aprons; and for fear this, together with the noise of their clamorous begging, should not sufficiently frighten the horses, they are very apt to let the gate slap full against you, before you are half way through, in their eager scuffle to snatch from each other the halfpence which you may have thrown out to them. I know two ladies who were one day very near being killed by these abominable tricks.

Thus five or six little idle creatures, who might be earning a trifle by knitting at home, who might be useful to the public by working in the field, and who might assist their families by learning to get their bread twenty honest ways, are suffered to lie about all day in the hope of a few chance halfpence, which, after all, they are by no means sure of getting. Indeed, when the neighboring gentlefolks found out that opening the gate was the family trade, they soon left off giving any thing. And I myself, though I used to take out a penny ready to give, had there been only one to receive it, when I saw a whole family established in so beggarly a trade, quietly put it back again into my pocket, and gave nothing at all. And so few travellers pass that way, that sometimes, after the whole family have lost a day, their gains do not Amount to twopence.

As Giles had a far greater taste for living by his wits than his work, he was at one time in hopes that his children might get a pretty penny by tumbling for the diversion of travellers, and he set about training them in that indecent practice; but, unluckily, the moors being level, the carriages travelled faster than the children tumbled. He envied those parents who lived on the London road, over the Wiltshire downs, which downs being very hilly, it enables the tumbler to keep pace with the traveller, till he sometimes extorts from the light and the unthinking a reward instead of a reproof. I beg leave, however, to put all gentlemen and ladies in mind, that such tricks are a kind of apprenticeship to the trades of begging and thieving; and that nothing is more injurious to good morals than to encourage the poor in any habits which may lead them to live upon chance.

Giles, to be sure, as his children grew older, began to train them to such other employments as the idle habits they had learned at the gate very properly qualified them for. The right of common, which some of the poor cottagers have in that part of the country, and which is doubtless a considerable advantage to many, was converted by Giles into the means of corrupting his whole family; for his children, as soon as they grew too big for the trade of begging at the gate, were promoted to the dignity of thieving on the moor.

Here he kept two or three asses, miserable creatures, which, if they had the good fortune to escape an untimely death by starving, did not fail to meet with it by beating. Some of the biggest boys were sent out with these lean and galled animals to carry sand or coals about the neighboring towns. Both sand and coals were often stolen before they got them to sell; or if not, they always took care to cheat in selling them. By long practice in this art, they grew so dexterous that they could give a pretty good guess how large a coal they could crib out of every bag before the buyer would be likely to miss it.

All their odd time was taken up under the pretence of watching these asses on the moor, or running after five or six halfstarved geese; but the truth is, these boys were only watching for an opportunity to steal an odd goose of their neighbor's, while they pretended to look after their own. They used also to pluck the quills or the down from these poor live creatures, or half milk a cow before the farmer's maid came with her pail. They all knew how to calculate to a minute what time to be down in a morning to let out their lank, hungry beasts, which they had turned over night into the farmer's field to steal a little good pasture. They contrived to get there just time enough to escape being caught in replacing the stakes they had pulled out for the cattle to get over. For Giles was a prudent, longheaded fellow; and wherever he stole food for his colts, took care never to steal stakes from the hedges at the same time. He had sense enough to know that the gain did not make up for the danger; he knew that a loose fagot, pulled from a neighbor's pile of wood after the family were gone to bed, answered the end better, and was not half the trouble.

Among the many trades which Giles professed, he sometimes practised that of a ratcatcher; but he was addicted to so many tricks, that he never followed the same trade long, for detection will sooner or later follow the bestconcerted villany. Whenever he was sent for to a farmhouse, his custom was to kill a few of the old rats, always taking care to leave a little stock of young ones alive sufficient to keep up the breed; "for," said he, "if I were to be such a fool as to clear a house or a barn at once, how would my trade be carried on?" And where any barn was overstocked, he used to borrow a few rats from thence, just to people a neighboring granary which had none; and he might have gone on till now, had he not unluckily been caught one evening emptying his cage of young rats under parson Wilson's barndoor.

This worthy minister, Mr. Wilson, used to pity the neglected children of Giles, as much as he blamed the wicked parents. He one day picked up Dick, who was far the best of Giles' bad boys. Dick was loitering about in a field behind the parson's garden, in search of a hen's nest, his mother having ordered him to bring home a few eggs that night, by hook or by crook, as Giles was resolved to have some pancakes for supper, though he knew that eggs were a penny apiece. Mr. Wilson had long been desirous of snatching some of this vagrant family from ruin; and his chief hopes were bent on Dick, as the least hackneyed in knavery. He had once given him a new pair of shoes, on his promising to go to school next Sunday; but no sooner had Rachel, the boy's mother, got the shoes into her clutches, than she pawned them for a bottle of gin, and ordered the boy to keep out of the parson's sight, and to be sure to play his marbles on Sunday, for the future, at the other end of the parish, and not near the churchyard.

Mr. Wilson, however, picked up the boy once more; for it was not his way to despair of any body. Dick was just going to take to his heels, as usual, for fear the old story of the shoes should be brought forward; but finding he could not get off, what does he do but run into a little puddle of muddy water which lay between him and the parson, that the sight of his naked feet might not bring on the dreaded subject. Now, it happened that Mr. Wilson was planting a little field of beans, so he thought this a good opportunity to employ Dick; and he told him he had got some pretty easy work for him. Dick did as he was bid; he willingly went to work, and readily began to plant his beans with dispatch and regularity, according to the directions given him.

While the boy was busily at work by himself, Giles happened to come by, having been skulking round the back way, to look over the parson's garden wall, to see if there was any thing worth climbing over for on the ensuing night. He spied Dick, and began to scold him for working for the stingy old parson; for Giles had a natural antipathy to whatever belonged to the church.

"What has he promised thee a day?" said he; "little enough, I dare say."

"He is not to pay me by the day," said Dick, "but says he will give me so much when I have planted this peck, and so much for the next."

"Oh, oh, that alters the case," said Giles. "One may, indeed, get a trifle by this sort of work. I hate your regular dayjobs, when one can't well avoid doing one's work for one's money. Come, give me a handful of the beans; I will teach thee how to plant when thou art paid for planting by the peck. All we have to do in that case is to dispatch the work as fast as we can, and get rid of the beans with all speed; and as to the seed coming up or not, that is no business of ours; we are paid for planting, not for growing. At the rate thou goest on, thou wouldst not get sixpence tonight. Come along, hurry away."

So saying, he took his hatfull of the seed, and where Dick had been ordered to set one bean, Giles buried a dozen; so the beans were soon out. But though the peck was emptied, the ground was unplanted. But cunning Giles knew this could not be found out till the time when the beans might be expected to come up; "and then, Dick," said he, "the snails and mice may go shares in the blame; or we can lay the fault on the rooks or the blackbirds." So saying, he sent the boy into the parsonage to receive his pay, taking care to secure about a quarter of the peck of beans for his own colt. He put both bag and beans into his own pocket to carry home, bidding Dick tell Mr. Wilson that he had planted the beans and lost the bag.

In the meantime Giles' other boys were busy in emptying the ponds and troutstreams in the neighboring manor. They would steal away the carp and tench when they were no bigger than gudgeons. By this untimely depredation they plundered the owner of his property, without enriching themselves. But the pleasure of mischief was reward enough.

These and a hundred other little thieveries they committed with such dexterity, that old Tom Crib, whose son was transported last assizes for sheepstealing, used to be often reproaching his boys, that Giles' sons were worth a hundred of such blockheads as he had; for scarce a night passed but Giles had some little comfortable thing for supper which his boys had pilfered in the day, while his undutiful dogs never stole any thing worth having. Giles, in the meantime, was busy in his way; but as busy as he was in laying nets, starting coveys, and training dogs, he always took care that his depredations should not be confined merely to game.

Giles' boys had never seen the inside of a church, and the father thought he knew his own interest better than to force them to it; for churchtime was the season of their harvest. Then the hens' nests were searched, a stray duck was clapped under the smockfrock, the tools which might have been left by chance in a farmyard were picked up, and all the neighboring pigeonhouses were thinned; so that Giles used to boast to tawny Rachel, his wife, that Sunday was to them the most profitable day in the week.

With her it was certainly the most laborious day, as she always did her washing and ironing on Sunday morning, it being, as she said, the only leisure day she had; for on the other days she went about the country telling fortunes, and selling dreambooks and wicked songs. Neither her husband's nor her children's clothes were ever mended, and if Sunday, her idle day, had not come about once in every week, it is likely they would never have been washed either. You might, however, see her as you were going to church smoothing her own rags on her best red cloak, which she always used for her ironingcloth on Sundays, for her cloak when she travelled, and for her blanket at night: such a wretched manager was Rachel.

Among her other articles of trade, one was to make and sell peppermint, and other distilled waters. These she had the cheap art of making without trouble and without expense, for she made them without herbs and without a still. Her way was, to fill so many quart bottles with plain water, putting a spoonful of mintwater in the mouth of each; these she corked down with rosin, carrying to each customer a vial of real distilled water to taste, by way of sample. This was so good that her bottles were commonly bought up without being opened; but if any suspicion arose, and she was forced to uncork a bottle, by the few drops of distilled water lying at top, she even then escaped detection, and took care to get out of reach before the bottle was opened a second time. She was too prudent ever to go twice to the same house.

THE UPRIGHT MAGISTRATE.

There is hardly any petty mischief that is not connected with the life of a poacher. Mr. Wilson was aware of this; he was not only a pious clergyman, but an upright justice. He used to say, that people who were truly conscientious, must be so in small things as well as in great ones, or they would destroy the effect of their own precepts, and their example would not be of general use. For this reason he never would accept of a hare or a partridge from any unqualified person in his parish. He did not content himself with shuffling the thing off by asking no questions, and pretending to take it for granted in a general way that the game was fairly come at; but he used to say, that by receiving the booty he connived at a crime, made himself a sharer in it, and if he gave a present to the man who brought it, he even tempted him to repeat the fault.

One day poor Jack Weston, an honest fellow in the neighborhood, whom Mr. Wilson had kindly visited and relieved in a long sickness, from which he had but just recovered, was brought before him as he was sitting on the justice's bench. Jack was accused of having knocked down a hare; and of all the birds in the air, who should the informer be but Black Giles the poacher. Mr. Wilson was grieved at the charge; he had a great regard for Jack, but he had a still greater regard for the law. The poor fellow pleaded guilty. He did not deny the fact, but said he did not consider it a crime, for he did not think game was private property, and he owned he had a strong temptation for doing what he had done, which he hoped would plead in his excuse. The justice desired to know what this temptation was.

"Sir," said the poor fellow, "you know I was given over this spring in a bad fever. I had no friend in the world but you, sir. Under God, you saved my life by your charitable relief; and I trust also you may have helped to save my soul by your prayers and your good advice; for, by the grace of God, I have turned over a new leaf since that sickness.

"I know I can never make you amends for all your goodness; but I thought it would be some comfort to my full heart if I could but once give you some little token of my gratitude. So I had trained a pair of nice turtledoves for Madam Wilson; but they were stolen from me, sir, and I do suspect Black Giles stole them. Yesterday morning, sir, as I was crawling out to my work, for I am still but very weak, a fine hare ran across my path. I did not stay to consider whether it was wrong to kill a hare, but I felt it was right to show my gratitude; so, sir, without a moment's thought, I did knock down the hare, which I was going to carry to your worship, because I knew madam was fond of hare. I am truly sorry for my fault, and will submit to whatever punishment your worship may please to inflict."

Mr. Wilson was much moved with this honest confession, and touched with the poor fellow's gratitude. What added to the effect of the story, was the weak condition, and pale, sickly looks of the offender. But this worthy magistrate never suffered his feelings to bias his integrity; he knew that he did not sit on that bench to indulge pity, but to administer justice. And while he was sorry for the offender, he would never justify the offence.

"John," said he, "I am surprised that you could for a moment forget that I never accept any gift which causes the giver to break a law. On Sunday I teach you from the pulpit the laws of God, whose minister I am. At present I fill the chair of the magistrate, to enforce and execute the laws of the land. Between these and the others there is more connection than you are aware. I thank you, John, for your affection to me, and I admire your gratitude; but I must not allow either affection or gratitude to be brought as a plea for a wrong action. It is not your business nor mine, John, to settle whether the gamelaws are good or bad. Till they are repealed we must obey them. Many, I doubt not, break these laws through ignorance, and many, I am certain, who would not dare to steal a goose or a turkey, make no scruple of knocking down a hare or a partridge. You will hereafter think yourself happy that this your first attempt has proved unsuccessful, as I trust you are too honest a fellow ever to intend to turn poacher. With poaching much more evil is connected: a habit of nightly depredation, a custom of prowling in the dark for prey, produces in time a disrelish for honest labor. He whose first offence was committed without much thought or evil intention, if he happens to succeed a few times in carrying off his booty undiscovered, grows bolder and bolder; and when he fancies there is no shame attending it, he very soon gets to persuade himself that there is also no sin. While some people pretend a scruple about stealing a sheep, they partly live by plundering of warrens. But remember, that the warrener pays a high rent, and that therefore his rabbits are as much his property as his sheep. Do not then deceive yourselves with these false distinctions. All property is sacred; and as the laws of the land are intended to fence in that property, he who brings up his children to break down any of these fences, brings them up to certain sin and ruin. He who begins with robbing orchards, rabbitwarrens, and fishponds, will probably end with horsestealing, or highway robbery. Poaching is a regular apprenticeship to bolder crimes. He whom I may commit as a boy to sit in the stocks for killing a partridge, may be likely to end at the gallows for killing a man.

"Observe, you who now hear me, the strictness and impartiality of justice. I know Giles to be a worthless fellow, yet it is my duty to take his information; I know Jack Weston to be an honest youth, yet I must be obliged to make him pay the penalty. Giles is a bad man, but he can prove this fact; Jack is a worthy lad, but he has committed this fault. I am sorry for you, Jack; but do not let it grieve you that Giles has played worse tricks a hundred times, and yet got off, while you were detected in the very first offence, for that would be grieving because you are not so great a rogue as Giles. At this moment you think your good luck is very unequal; but all this will one day turn out in your favor. Giles is not the more a favorite of heaven because he has hitherto escaped Botany Bay or the hulks; nor is it any mark of God's displeasure against you, John, that you were found out in your very first attempt."

Here the good justice left off speaking, and no one could contradict the truth of what he had said. Weston humbly submitted to his sentence, but he was very poor, and knew not where to raise the money to pay his fine. His character had always been so fair, that several farmers present kindly agreed to advance a trifle each, to prevent his being sent to prison, and he thankfully promised to work out the debt. The justice himself, though he could not soften the law, yet showed Weston so much kindness, that he was enabled, before the year was out, to get out of this difficulty. He began to think more seriously than he had ever yet done, and grew to abhor poaching, not merely from fear but from principle.

We shall soon see whether poaching Giles always got off so successfully. Here we have seen that worldly prosperity is no sure sign of goodness; and that "the triumphing of the wicked is short," will appear in the second part of the Poacher, containing the entertaining story of the Widow Brown's Appletree.

HISTORY OF WIDOW BROWN'S APPLETREE.

I think my readers are so well acquainted with Black Giles the poacher, that they will not expect to hear any great good, either of Giles himself, his wife Rachel, or any of their family. I am sorry to expose their tricks, but it is their fault, not mine. If I pretend to speak about people at all, I must tell the truth. I am sure, if folks would but turn about and mend, it would be a thousand times pleasanter to me to write their histories; as it is no comfort to tell of any body's faults. If the world would but grow good, I should be glad enough to tell of it; but till it really becomes so, I must go on describing it as it is; otherwise I should only mislead my readers, instead of instructing them. It is the duty of a faithful historian to relate the evil with the good.

As to Giles and his boys, I am sure old widow Brown has good reason to remember their dexterity. Poor woman, she had a fine little bed of onions in her neat and wellkept garden; she was very fond of her onions, and many a rheumatism has she caught by kneeling down to weed them in a damp day, notwithstanding the little flannel cloak and the bit of an old mat which Madam Wilson gave her, because the old woman would needs weed in wet weather. Her onions she always carefully treasured up for her winter's store; for an onion makes a little broth very relishing, and is, indeed, the only savory thing poor people are used to get.

She had also a small orchard, containing about a dozen appletrees, with which, in a good year, she has been known to make a couple of barrels of cider, which she sold to her landlord towards paying her rent, besides having a little keg which she was able to keep back for her own drinking.

Well, would you believe it? Giles and his boys marked both onions and apples for their own. Indeed, a man who stole so many rabbits from the warren, was likely enough to steal onions for sauce. One day when the widow was abroad on a little business, Giles and his boys made a clear riddance of the onionbed; and when they had pulled up every single onion, they then turned a couple of pigs into the garden, who, allured by the smell, tore up the bed in such a manner, that the widow, when she came home, had not the least doubt but the pigs had been the thieves. To confirm this opinion, they took care to leave the little hatch half open at one end of the garden, and to break down a bit of a fence at the other end.

I wonder how any body can find in his heart not to pity and respect poor old widows. There is something so forlorn and helpless in their condition, that methinks it is a call on every body, men, women, and children, to do them all the kind services that fall in their way. Surely, their having no one to take their part, is an additional reason for kindhearted people not to hurt and oppress them. But it was this very reason which led Giles to do this woman an injury. With what a touching simplicity it is recorded in Scripture, of the youth whom our blessed Saviour raised from the dead, that he was the only son of his mother, and she was a widow.

It happened, unluckily for poor widow Brown, that her cottage stood quite alone. On several mornings togetherfor roguery gets up much earlier than industryGiles and his boys stole regularly into her orchard, followed by their jackasses. She was so deaf that she could not hear the asses, if they had brayed ever so loud, and to this Giles trusted; for he was very cautious in his rogueries, since he could not otherwise have contrived so long to keep out of prison; for though he was almost always suspected, he had seldom been taken up, and never convicted. The boys used to fill their bags, load their asses, and then march off; and if, in their way to the town where the apples were to be sold, they chanced to pass by one of their neighbors who might be likely to suspect them, they then all at once began to scream out, "Buy my coal? buy my sand?"

Besides the trees in her orchard, poor widow Brown had in her small garden one appletree particularly fine; it was a redstreak, so tempting and so lovely that Giles' family had watched it with longing eyes, till at last they resolved on a plan for carrying off all this fine fruit in their bags. But it was a nice point to manage. The tree stood directly under her chamber window, so that there was some danger that she might spy them at the work. They therefore determined to wait till the next Sunday morning, when they knew she would not fail to be at church. Sunday came; it was a lone house, as I said before, and most of the parish were safe at church. In a trice the tree was cleared, the bags were filled, the asses were whipped, the thieves were off, the coast was clear, and all was safe and quiet by the time the sermon was over.

Unluckily, however, it happened, that this tree was so beautiful, and the fruit so fine, that the people, as they used to pass to and from church, were very apt to stop and admire widow Brown's redstreaks; and some of the farmers rather envied her, that in that scarce season, when they hardly expected to make a pie out of a large orchard, she was likely to make a cask of cider from a single tree. I am afraid, indeed, if I must speak out, she herself rather set her heart too much upon this fruit, and had felt as much pride in her tree as gratitude to a good Providence for it; but this failing of hers was no excuse for Giles. The covetousness of this thief had for once got the better of his caution; the tree was too completely stripped, though the youngest boy Dick did beg hard that his father would leave the poor old woman enough for a few dumplings; and when Giles ordered Dick in his turn to shake the tree, the boy did it so gently that hardly any apples fell, for which he got a good stroke of the stick with which the old man was beating down the apples.

The neighbors, on their return from church, stopped as usual; but it wasnot, alas, to admire the apples, for apples there were none left, but to lament the robbery, and console the widow. Meantime the redstreaks were safely lodged in Giles' hovel, under a few bundles of hay, which he had contrived to pull from the farmer's mow the night before, for the use of his jackasses.

Such a stir, however, began to be made about the widow's appletree, that Giles, who knew how much his character laid him open to suspicion, as soon as he saw the people safe in church again in the afternoon, ordered his boys to carry each a hatful of the apples, and thrust them in at a little casement window, which happened to be open in the house of Samuel Price, a very honest carpenter in that parish, who was at church with his whole family. Giles' plan, by this contrivance, was to lay the theft on Price's sons, in case the thing should come to be further inquired into. Here Dick put in a word, and begged and prayed his father not to force them to carry the apples to Price's. But all that he got by his begging was such a knock as had nearly laid him on the earth.

"What, you cowardly rascal," said Giles, "you will go and peach, I suppose, and get your father sent to jail."

Poor widow Brown, though her trouble had made her still weaker than she was, went to church again in the afternoon; indeed, she rightly thought that her being in trouble was a new reason why she ought to go. During the service she tried with all her might not to think of her redstreaks; and whenever they would come into her head, she took up her prayerbook directly, and so she forgot them a little; and, indeed, she found herself much easier when she came out of the church than when she went inan effect so commonly produced by prayer, that methinks it is a pity people do not try it oftener.

Now it happened oddly enough, that on that Sunday, of all the Sundays in the year, the widow should call in to rest a little at Samuel Price's, to tell over again the lamentable story of the apples, and to consult with him how the thief might be brought to justice. But O, reader, guess, if you can, for I am sure I cannot tell you, what was her surprise, when, on going into Samuel Price's kitchen, she saw her own redstreaks lying in the window! The apples were of a sort too remarkable for color, shape, and size, to be mistaken. There was not such another tree in the parish.

Widow Brown immediately screamed out, "'Lasaday! as sure as can be, here are my redstreaks; I can swear to them in any court." Samuel Price, who believed his sons to be as honest as himself, was shocked and troubled at the sight. He knew he had no redstreaks of his own; he knew there were no apples in the window when he went to church; he did verily believe these apples to be the widow's. But how they came there he could not possibly guess. He called for Tom, the only one of his sons who now lived at home. Tom was at the Sundayschool, which he had never once missed since Mr. Wilson the minister had set one up in the parish. Was such a boy likely to do such a deed?

A crowd had by this time got about Price's door, among which was Giles and his boys, who had already taken care to spread the news that Tom Price was the thief. Most people were unwilling to believe it. His character was very good, but appearances were strongly against him. Mr. Wilson now came in. He was much concerned that Tom Price, the best boy in his school, should stand accused of such a crime. He sent for the boy, examined, and crossexamined him. No marks of guilt appeared. But still, though he pleaded not guilty, there lay the redstreaks in his father's window.

All the idle fellows in the place, who were most likely to have committed such a theft themselves, fell with great vengeance on poor Tom. The wicked seldom give any quarter. "This is one of your sanctified ones!" cried they. "This was all the good that Sundayschools did! For their parts, they never saw any good come by religion. Sunday was the only day for a little pastime; and if poor boys must be shut up with their godly books, when they ought to be out taking a little pleasure, it was no wonder they made themselves amends by such tricks."

Another said he should like to see parson Wilson's righteous one well whipped. A third hoped he would be clapped in the stocks for a young hypocrite as he was; while old Giles, who thought it was the only way to avoid suspicion by being more violent than the rest, declared, that "he hoped the young dog would be transported for life."

Mr. Wilson was too wise and too just to proceed against Tom without full proof. He declared the crime was a very heavy one, and he feared that heavy must be the punishment. Tom, who knew his own innocence, earnestly prayed to God that it might be made to appear as clear as the noonday; and very fervent were his secret devotions on that night.

Black Giles passed his night in a very different manner. He set off as soon as it was dark, with his sons and their jackasses laden with their stolen goods. As such a cry was raised about the apples, he did not think it safe to keep them longer at home, but resolved to go and sell them at the next town; borrowing without leave a lame colt out of the moor to assist in carrying off his booty.

Giles and his eldest sons had rare sport all the way in thinking, that while they were enjoying the profit of their plunder, Tom Price would be whipped round the marketplace at least, if not sent beyond sea. But the younger boy, Dick, who had naturally a tender heart, though hardened by his long familiarity with sin, could not help crying when he thought that Tom Price might perhaps be transported for a crime which he himself had helped to commit. He had had no compunction about the robbery, for he had not been instructed in the great principles of truth and justice; nor would he, therefore, perhaps have had much remorse about accusing an innocent boy. But, though utterly devoid of principle, he had some remains of natural feeling and of gratitude. Tom Price had often given him a bit of his own bread and cheese; and once, when Dick was like to be drowned, Tom had jumped into the pond with his clothes on, and saved his life, when he was just sinking: the remembrance of all this made his heart heavy. He said nothing; but, as he trotted, barefoot, after the asses, he heard his father and brothers laugh at having outwitted the godly ones; and he grieved to think how poor Tom would suffer for his wickedness, yet fear kept him silent: they called him sulky dog, and lashed the asses till they bled.

In the meantime, Tom Price kept up his spirits as well as he could. He worked hard all day, and prayed heartily night and morning.

"It is true," said he to himself, "I am not guilty of this sin; but let this accusation set me on examining myself, and truly repenting of all my other sins; for I find enough to repent of, though I thank God I did not steal the widow's apples."

At length Sunday came, and Tom went to school as usual. As soon as he walked in, there was a great deal of whispering and laughing among the worst of the boys; and he overheard them say, "Who would have thought it? This is master's favorite! This is parson Wilson's sober Tommy! We sha'n't have Tommy thrown in our teeth again, if we go to get a birdsnest, or gather a few nuts on a Sunday." "Your demure ones are always hypocrites," says another. "The still sow sucks all the milk," says a third.

Giles' family had always kept clear of the school. Dick, indeed, had sometimes wished to go: not that he had much sense of sin, or desire after goodness, but he thought if he could once read, he might rise in the world, and not be forced to drive asses all his life. Through this whole Saturday night he could not sleep. He longed to know what would be done to Tom. He began to wish to go to school, but he had not couragesin is very cowardly: so, on the Sunday morning, he went and sat himself down under the churchwall. Mr. Wilson passed by. It was not his way to reject the most wicked, till he had tried every means to bring them over; and even then he pitied and prayed for them. He had, indeed, long left off talking to Giles' sons; but, seeing Dick sitting by himself, he once more spoke to him, desired him to leave off his vagabond life, and go with him into the school. The boy hung down his head, but made no answer. He did not, however, either rise up and run away, or look sulky, as he used to do. The minister desired him once more to go.

"Sir," said the boy, "I can't go; I am so big I am ashamed."

"The bigger you are, the less time you have to lose."

"But, sir, I can't read."

"Then it is high time you should learn."

"I should be ashamed to begin to learn my letters."

"The shame is not in beginning to learn them, but in being contented never to know them."

"But, sir, I am so ragged."

"God looks at the heart, and not at the coat."

"But, sir, I have no shoes and stockings."

"So much the worse; I remember who gave you both." Here Dick colored. "It is bad to want shoes and stockings; but still, if you can drive your asses a dozen miles without them, you may certainly walk a hundred yards to school without them."

"But, sir, the good boys will hate me, and wont speak to me."

"Good boys hate nobody; and as to not speaking to you, to be sure they will not keep you company while you go on in your present evil courses; but as soon as they see you wish to reform, they will help you, and pity you, and teach you; so come along." Here Mr. Wilson took this dirty boy by the hand, and gently pulled him forward, kindly talking to him all the way.

How the whole school stared to see Dick Giles come in! No one, however, dared to say what he thought. The business went on, and Dick slunk into a corner, partly to hide his rags, and partly to hide his sin; for last Sunday's transactions sat heavy on his heart, not because he had stolen the apples, but because Tom Price had been accused. This, I say, made him slink behind. Poor boy, he little thought there was One saw him who sees all things, and from whose eye no hole or corner can hide the sinner; for he is about our bed, and about our paths, and spieth out all our ways.

It was the custom in that school for the master, who was a good and wise man, to mark down in his pocketbook all the events of the week, that he might turn them to some account in his Sunday evening instructions: such as any useful story in the newspaper, any account of boys being drowned as they were out in a pleasureboat on Sundays, any sudden death in the parish, or any other remarkable visitation of Providence; insomuch, that many young people in the place, who did not belong to the school, and many parents, also, used to drop in for an hour on a Sunday evening, when they were sure to hear something profitable. The minister greatly approved this practice, and often called in himself, which was a great support to the master, and encouragement to the people.

The master had taken a deep concern in the story of widow Brown's appletree. He could not believe Tom Price was guilty, nor dared he pronounce him innocent; but he resolved to turn the instructions of the present evening to this subject. He began thus: "My dear boys, however light some of you may make of robbing an orchard, yet I have often told you there is no such thing as a little sin, if it be wilful or habitual. I wish now to explain to you, also, that there is hardly such a thing as a single solitary sin. You know I teach you not merely to repeat the commandments as an exercise for your memory, but as a rule for your conduct. If you were to come here on a Sunday only to learn to read and spell, I should think that was not employing God's day for God's work; but I teach you to read, that you may, by this means, so understand the Bible and the catechism, as to make every text in the one, and every question and answer in the other, to be so fixed in your hearts, that they may bring forth the fruits of good living."

MASTER. "How many commandments are there?"

BOY. "Ten."

MASTER. "How many did that boy break who stole widow Brown's apples?"

BOY. "Only one, master; the eighth."

MASTER. "What is the eighth?"

BOY. "Thou shalt not steal."

MASTER. "And you are very sure that this was the only one he broke? Now, suppose I could prove to you that he probably broke, not less than six out of those ten commandments, which the great Lord of heaven himself stooped down from his eternal glory to deliver to men, would you not then think it a terrible thing to steal, whether apples or guineas?"

BOY. "Yes, master."

MASTER. "I will put the case. Some wicked boy has robbed widow Brown's orchard." Here the eyes of every one were turned on poor Tom Price, except those of Dick Giles, who fixed his on the ground. "I accuse no one," continued the master; "Tom Price is a good boy, and was not missing at the time of the robbery: these are two reasons why I presume he is innocent; but whoever it was, you allow that by stealing these apples he broke the eighth commandment?"

BOY. "Yes, master."

MASTER. "On what day were these apples stolen?"

BOY. "On Sunday."

MASTER. "What is the fourth commandment?"

BOY. "Thou shalt keep holy the Sabbathday."

MASTER, "Does that person keep holy the Sabbathday, who loiters in an orchard on Sunday when he should be at church, and steals apples when he ought to be at prayer?"

BOY. "No, master."

MASTER. "What command does he break?"

BOY. "The fourth."

MASTER. "Suppose this boy had parents, who had sent him to church, and that he had disobeyed them by not going; would that be keeping the fifth commandment?"

BOY. "No, master; for the fifth commandment says, 'Thou shalt honor thy father and thy mother.'"

This was the only part in the case in which poor Dick Giles' heart did not smite him; for he knew he had disobeyed no fatherfor his father, alas, was still more wicked than himself, and had brought him up to commit the sin. But what a wretched comfort was this. The master went on.

MASTER. "Suppose this boy earnestly coveted this fruit, though it belonged to another person; would that be right?"

BOY. "No, master; for the tenth commandment says, 'Thou shalt not covet.'"

MASTER. "Very well. Here are four of God's positive commands already broken. Now, do you think thieves ever scruple to use wicked words?"

BOY. "I am afraid not, master."

Here Dick Giles was not so hardened but that he remembered how many curses had passed between him and his father while they were filling the bags, and he was afraid to look up. The master went on.

"I will now go one step further. If the thief to all his other sins has added that of accusing the innocent to save himselfif he should break the ninth commandment, by bearing false witness against a harmless neighbor, then six commandments are broken for an apple! But if it be otherwise, if Tom Price should be found guilty, it is not his good character shall save him. I shall shed tears over him, but punish him I must, and that severely."

"No, that you sha'n't," roared out Dick Giles, who sprung from his hidingplace, fell on his knees, and burst out a crying. "Tom Price is as good a boy as ever lived; it was father and I who stole the apples."

It would have done your heart good to have seen the joy of the master, the modest blushes of Tom Price, and the satisfaction of every honest boy in the school. All shook hands with Tom, and even Dick got some portion of pity. I wish I had room to give my readers the moving exhortation which the master gave. But while Mr. Wilson left the guilty boy to the management of the master, he thought it became him, as a minister and a magistrate, to go to the extent of the law in punishing the father.

Early on Monday morning, he sent to apprehend Giles. In the meantime, Mr. Wilson was sent for to a gardener's house, two miles distant, to attend a man who was dying. This was a duty to which all others gave way, in his mind. He set out directly; but what was his surprise, on his arrival, to see, on a little bed on the floor, poaching Giles lying, in all the agonies of death! Jack Weston, a poor young man, against whom Giles had informed for killing a hare, was kneeling by him, offering him some broth, and talking to him in the kindest manner. Mr. Wilson begged to know the meaning of all this; and Jack Weston spoke as follows:

"At four this morning, as I was going out to mow, passing under the high wall of this garden, I heard a most dismal moaning. The nearer I came, the more dismal it grew. At last, who should I see but poor Giles, groaning and struggling under a quantity of bricks and stones, but not able to stir. The day before, he had marked a fine large net on this old wall, and resolved to steal it; for he thought it might do as well to catch partridges as to preserve cherries: so, sir, standing on the very top of this wall, and tugging with all his might to loosen the net from the hooks which fastened it, down came Giles, net, wall, and all; for the wall was gone to decay. It was very high, indeed, and poor Giles not only broke his thigh, but has got a terrible blow on his brain, and is bruised all over like a mummy.

"On seeing me, sir, poor Giles cried out, 'Oh, Jack, I did try to ruin thee by lodging that information, and now thou wilt be revenged by letting me lie here and perish.'

"'God forbid, Giles,' cried I; 'thou shalt see what sort of revenge a Christian takes.' So, sir, I sent off the gardener's boy to fetch a surgeon, while I scampered home, and brought, on my back, this bit of a hammock, which is indeed my own bed, and put Giles upon it: we then lifted him up, bed and all, as tenderly as if he had been a gentleman, and brought him in here. My wife has just brought him a drop of nice broth; and now, sir, as I have done what I could for his poor perishing body, it was I who took the liberty to send to you to come and try to help his poor soul, for the doctor says he can't live."

Mr. Wilson could not help saying to himself, "Such an action as this is worth a whole volume of comments on that precept of our blessed Master, 'Love your enemies: do good to them that hate you.'"

Giles' dying groans confirmed the sad account Weston had just given. The poor wretch could neither pray himself, nor attend to the minister. He could only cry out, "Oh, sir, what will become of me? I don't know how to repent. O my poor wicked children! Sir, I have bred them all up in sin and ignorance. Have mercy on them, sir; let me not meet them in the place of torment to which I am going. Lord, grant them that time for repentance which I have thrown away!" He languished a few days, and died in great miserya fresh and sad instance, that people who abuse the grace of God, and resist his Spirit, find it difficult to repent when they will.

Except the minister and Jack Western, no one came to see poor Giles, besides Tommy Price, who had been so sadly wronged by him. Tom often brought him his own rice and milk or appledumpling; and Giles, ignorant and depraved as he was, often cried out that "he thought now there must be some truth in religion, since it taught even a boy to deny himself, and to forgive an injury." Mr. Wilson, the next Sunday, made a moving discourse on the danger of what are called "petty offences." This, together with the awful death of Giles, produced such an effect, that no poacher has been able to show his head in that parish ever since.

TAWYNEY RACHEL;

OR, THE FORTUNETELLER.
WITH SOME ACCOUNT OF DREAMS, OMENS, AND CONJURERS

BY HANNAH MORE.

Tawney Rachel was the wife of poaching Giles. There seemed to be a conspiracy in Giles' whole family to maintain themselves by tricks and pilfering. Regular labor and honest industry did not suit their idle habits. They had a sort of genius at finding out every unlawful means to support a vagabond life. Rachel travelled the country with a basket on her arm. She pretended to get her bread by selling laces, cabbagenets, ballads, and historybooks, and used to buy old rags and rabbit skins. Many honest people trade in these things, and I am sure I do not mean to say a word against honest people, let them trade in what they will. But Rachel only made this traffic a pretence for getting admittance into farmers' kitchens, in order to tell fortunes.

She was continually practising on the credulity of silly girls; and took advantage of their ignorance to cheat and deceive them. Many an innocent servant has she caused to be suspected of a robbery, while she herself, perhaps, was in league with the thief. Many a harmless maid has she brought to ruin by contriving plots and events herself, and then pretending to foretell them. She had not, to be sure, the power of really foretelling things, because she had no power of seeing into futurity; but she had the art sometimes to bring them about according as she had foretold them. So she got that credit for her wisdom which really belonged to her wickedness.

Rachel was also a famous interpreter of dreams, and could distinguish exactly between the fate of any two persons who happened to have a mole on the right or the left cheek. She had a cunning way of getting herself off when any of her prophecies failed. When she explained a dream according to the natural appearance of things, and it did not come to pass, then she would get out of that scrape by saying, that "this sort of dreams went by contraries." Now, of two very opposite things the chance always is, that one of them may turn out to be true; so in either case she kept up the cheat.

Rachel, in one of her rambles, stopped at the house of farmer Jenkins. She contrived to call when she knew the master of the house was from home, which indeed was her usual way. She knocked at the door. The maids being out haymaking, Mrs. Jenkins went to open it herself. Rachel asked her if she would please to let her light her pipe. This was a common pretence, when she could find no other way of getting into a house. While she was filling her pipe, she looked at Mrs. Jenkins, and said she could tell her some good fortune. The farmer's wife, who was a very inoffensive, but a weak and superstitious woman, was curious to know what she meant. Rachel then looked about very carefully, and shutting the door with a mysterious air, asked her if she was sure nobody would hear them. This appearance of mystery was at once delightful and terrifying to Mrs. Jenkins, who, with trembling agitation, bade the cunning woman speak out.

"Then," said Rachel in a solemn whisper, "there is to my certain knowledge a pot of money hid under one of the stones in your cellar."

"Indeed," said Mrs. Jenkins, "it is impossible; for now I think of it, I dreamed last night I was in prison for debt."

"Did you indeed?" said Rachel, "that is quite surprising. Did you dream before twelve o'clock, or after?"

"O, it was this morning, just before I awoke."

"Then I am sure it is true, for morning dreams always go by contraries," cried Rachel. "How lucky it was you dreamed it so late."

Mrs. Jenkins could hardly contain her joy, and asked how the money was to be come at.

"There is but one way," said Rachel; "I must go into the cellar. I know by my art under which stone it lies, but I must not tell."

Then they both went down into the cellar, but Rachel refused to point at the stone, unless Mrs. Jenkins would put five pieces of gold into a basin, and do as she directed. The simple woman, instead of turning her out of doors for a cheat, did as she was bid. She put the guineas into a basin, which she gave into Rachel's hand. Rachel strewed some white powder over the gold, muttered some barbarous words, and pretended to perform the black art. She then told Mrs. Jenkins to put the basin quietly down within the cellar; telling her, that if she offered to look into it, or even to speak a word, the charm would be broken. She also directed her to lock the cellardoor, and on no pretence to open it in less than fortyeight hours.

"If," added she, "you closely follow these directions, then, by the power of my art, you will find the basin conveyed to the very stone under which the money lies hid, and a fine treasure it will be." Mrs. Jenkins, who believed every word the woman said, did exactly as she was told, and Rachel took her leave with a handsome reward.

When farmer Jenkins came home, he desired his wife to draw him a cup of cider; this she put off doing so long that he began to be displeased. At last she begged he would drink a little beer instead. He insisted on knowing the reason, and when at last he grew angry, she told him all that had passed; and owned that as the pot of gold happened to be in the cidercellar, she did not dare to open the door, as she was sure it would break the charm. "And it would be a pity, you know," said she, "to lose a good fortune for the sake of a draught of cider."

The farmer, who was not so easily imposed upon, suspected a trick. He demanded the key, and went and opened the cellardoor; there he found the basin, and in it five round pieces of tin covered with powder. Mrs. Jenkins burst out a crying; but the farmer thought of nothing but getting a warrant to apprehend the cunning woman. Indeed, she well proved her claim to that name, when she insisted that the cellardoor might be kept locked till she had time to get out of the reach of all pursuit.

Poor Sally Evans. I am sure she rued the day that ever she listened to a fortuneteller. Sally was as harmless a girl as ever churned a pound of butter; but Sally was ignorant and superstitious. She delighted in dreambooks, and had consulted all the cunning women in the country to tell her whether the two moles on her cheek denoted that she was to have two husbands, or only two children. If she picked up an old horseshoe going to church, she was sure that would be a lucky week. She never made a blackpudding without borrowing one of the parson's old wigs to hang in the chimney, firmly believing there were no other means to preserve them from bursting.

She would never go to bed on Midsummereve without sticking up in her room the wellknown plant called Midsummermen, as the bending of the leaves to the right or to the left, would not fail to tell her whether Jacob, of whom we shall speak presently, was true or false. She would rather go five miles about than pass near a churchyard at night. Every seventh year she would not eat beans, because they grew downward in the pod, instead of upward; and she would rather have gone with her gown open than have taken a pin of an old woman, for fear of being bewitched.

Poor Sally had so many unlucky days in her calendar, that a large portion of her time became of little use, because on these days she did not dare set about any new work. And she would have refused the best offer in the country if made to her on a Friday, which she thought so unlucky a day, that she often said what a pity it was that there was any Friday in the week. Sally had twenty pounds left her by her grandmother. She had long been courted by Jacob, a sober lad, with whom she lived a fellowservant at a creditable farmer's. Honest Jacob, like his namesake of old, thought it little to wait seven years to get this damsel to wife, because of the love he bore her, for Sally had promised to marry him when he could match her twenty pounds with another of his own.

Now, there was one Robert, a rambling, idle young gardener, who, instead of sitting down steadily in one place, used to roam about the country, and do odd jobs where he could get them. No one understood any thing about him, except that he was a downlooking fellow, who came nobody knew whence, and got his bread nobody knew how, and never had a penny in his pocket. Robert, who was now in the neighborhood, happened to hear of Sally Evans and her twenty pounds. He immediately conceived a longing desire for the latter. So he went to his old friend Rachel, told her all he had heard of Sally, and promised if she could bring about a marriage between them, she should go shares in the money.

Rachel undertook the business. She set off to the farmhouse, and fell to singing one of her most enticing songs just under the dairy window. Sally was so struck with the pretty tune, which was unhappily used, as is too often the case, to set off some very loose words, that she jumped up, dropped the skimming dish into the cream, and ran out to buy the song.

While she stooped down to rummage the basket for those songs which had the most tragical picturesfor Sally had a most tender heart, and delighted in whatever was mournfulRachel looked steadfastly in her face, and told her she knew by her art that she was born to good fortune, but advised her not to throw herself away. "These two moles on your cheek," added she, "show you are in some danger."

"Do they denote husbands or children?" cried Sally, starting up, and letting fall the song of the Children in the Wood.

"Husbands," muttered Rachel.

"Alas, poor Jacob," said Sally mournfully; "then he will die first, wont he?"

"Mum for that," quoth the fortuneteller; "I will say no more."

Sally was impatient, but the more curiosity she discovered, the more mystery Rachel affected. At last she said, "If you will cross my hand with a piece of silver, I will tell you your fortune. By the power of my art, I can do this three ways: by cards, by the lines of your hand, or by turning a cup of teagrounds; which will you have?"

"O, all, all," cried Sally, looking up with reverence to this sunburnt oracle of wisdom, who knew no less than three different ways of diving into the secrets of futurity. Alas, persons of better sense than Sally have been so taken in; the more is the pity.

The poor girl said she would run up stairs to her little box, where she kept her money tied up in a bit of an old glove, and would bring down a bright queen Anne's sixpence very crooked. "I am sure," added she, "it is a lucky one, for it cured me of a very bad ague last spring, by only laying it nine nights under my pillow, without speaking a word. But then you must know what gave virtue to this sixpence was, that it had belonged to three young men of the name of John; I am sure I had work enough to get it. But true it is, it certainly cured me. It must be the sixpence you know, for I am sure I did nothing else for my ague, except indeed taking some bitter stuff every three hours, which the doctor called bark. To be sure, I lost my ague soon after I took it, but I am certain it was owing to the crooked sixpence, and not to the bark. And so, good woman, you may come in if you will, for there is not a soul in the house but me." This was the very thing Rachel wanted to know, and very glad she was to learn it.

While Sally was above stairs untying her glove, Rachel slipped into the parlor, took a small silver cup from the beaufet, and clapped it into her pocket. Sally ran down lamenting that she had lost her sixpence, which she verily believed was owing to her having put it into a left glove, instead of a right one. Rachel comforted her by saying, that "if she gave her two plain ones instead, the charm would work just as well."

Simple Sally thought herself happy to be let off so easily, never calculating that a smooth shilling was worth two crooked sixpences. But this skill was a part of the black art in which Rachel excelled. She took the money, and began to examine the lines of Sally's left hand. She bit her withered lip, shook her head, and bade her, poor dupe, beware of a young man, who had black hair.

"No, indeed," cried Sally, all in a fright, "you mean black eyes, for our Jacob has got brown hair; 'tis his eyes that are black."

"That is the very thing I was going to say," muttered Rachel; "I meant eyes, though I said hair; for I know his hair is as brown as a chesnut, and his eyes as black as a sloe."

"So they are, sure enough," cried Sally; "how in the world could you know that?" forgetting that she herself had just told her so. And it is thus that these hags pick out of the credulous all which they afterwards pretend to reveal to them.

"Oh, I know a pretty deal more than that," said Rachel, "but you must be aware of this man."

"Why so?" cried Sally with great quickness.

"Because," answered Rachel, "you are fated to marry a man worth a hundred of him, who has grey eyes, light hair, and a stoop in the shoulders."

"No, indeed, but I can't," said Sally; "I have promised Jacob, and Jacob I will marry."

"You cannot, child," returned Rachel, in a solemn tone; "it is out of your power; you are fated to marry the grey eyes and light hair."

"Nay, indeed," said Sally, sighing deeply, "if I am fated, I must; I know there is no resisting one's fate." This is a common cant with poor deluded girls, who are not aware that they themselves make their fate by their folly, and then complain there is no resisting it.

"What can I do?" said Sally.

"I will tell you that too," said Rachel. "You must take a walk next Sunday afternoon to the churchyard, and the first man you meet in a blue coat, with a large posy of pinks and southernwood in his bosom, sitting on the churchyard wall, about seven o'clock, he will be the man."

"Provided," said Sally, much disturbed, "that he has grey eyes, and stoops."

"O, to be sure," said Rachel; "otherwise it is not the right man."

"But if I should mistake," said Sally; "for two men may happen to have a coat and eyes of the same color."

"To prevent that," replied Rachel, "if it is the right man, the two first letters of his name will be R.P. This man has got money beyond sea."

"Oh, I do not value his money," said Sally, with tears in her eyes, "for I love Jacob better than house or land; but if I am fated to marry another, I can't help it; you know there is no struggling against my fate."

Poor Sally thought of nothing and dreamed of nothing all the week but the blue coat and the grey eyes. She made a hundred blunders at her work. She put her rennet into the butterpan, and her skimming dish into the cheesetub. She gave the curds to the hogs, and put the whey into the vats. She put her little knife out of her pocket, for fear it should cut love; and would not stay in the kitchen, if there was not an even number of people, lest it should break the charm. She grew cold and mysterious in her behavior to faithful Jacob, whom she truly loved. But the more she thought of the fortuneteller, the more she was convinced that brown hair and black eyes were not what she was fated to marry, and therefore, though she trembled to think it, Jacob could not be the man.

On Sunday she was too uneasy to go to church; for poor Sally had never been taught, that her being uneasy was only a fresh reason why she ought to go thither. She spent the whole afternoon in her little garret, dressing in all her best. First she put on her red ribbon, which she had bought at last Lammas fair; then she recollected that red was an unlucky color, and changed it for a blue ribbon, tied in a true lover's knot; but suddenly calling to mind that poor Jacob had bought this knot for her of a pedlar at the door, and that she had promised to wear it for his sake, her heart smote her, and she laid it by, sighing to think she was not fated to marry the man who had given it to her.

When she had looked at herself twenty times in the glassfor one vain action always brings on anothershe set off, trembling and quaking every step she went. She walked eagerly towards the churchyard, not daring to look to the right or left, for fear she should spy Jacob, who would have offered to walk with her, and so have spoiled all. As soon as she came within sight of the wall, she spied a man sitting upon it. Her heart beat violently. She looked again; but alas, the stranger not only had on a black coat, but neither hair nor eyes answered the description. She now happened to cast her eyes on the churchclock, and found she was two hours before her time. This was some comfort. She walked away and got rid of the two hours as well as she could, paying great attention as she went not to walk over any straws which lay across, and carefully looking to see if there were never an old horseshoe in the way, that infallible symptom of good fortune.

While the clock was striking seven, she returned to the churchyard, and, O the wonderful power of fortunetellers, there she saw him! there sat the very man: his hair as light as flax, his eyes as blue as buttermilk, and his shoulders as round as a tub. Every tittle agreed, to the very nosegay in his waistcoat buttonhole. At first, indeed, she thought it had been sweetbriar, and glad to catch at a straw, whispered to herself, It is not he, and I shall marry Jacob still; but on looking again, she saw it was southernwood plain enough, and that of course all was over. The man accosted her with some very nonsensical, but too acceptable compliments. Sally was naturally a modest girl, and but for Rachel's wicked arts, would not have had courage to talk with a strange man; but how could she resist her fate, you know? After a little discourse, she asked him with a trembling heart, what might be his name.

"Robert Price, at your service," was the answer.

"Robert Price! that is R.P. as sure as I am alive, and the fortuneteller was a witch. It is all out; it is all out! O the wonderful art of fortunetellers!"

The little sleep she had that night was disturbed with dreams of graves, and ghosts, and funerals; but as they were morning dreams, she knew those always went by contraries, and that a funeral denoted a wedding. Still, a sigh would now and then heave, to think that in that wedding Jacob could have no part. Such of my readers as know the power which superstition has over the weak and credulous mind, scarcely need be told, that poor Sally's unhappiness was soon completed. She forgot all her vows to Jacob; she at once forsook an honest man whom she loved, and consented to marry a stranger, of whom she knew nothing, from a ridiculous notion that she was compelled to do so by a decree which she had it not in her power to resist. She married this Robert Price, the strange gardener, whom she soon found to be very worthless, and very much in debt. He had no such thing as "money beyond sea," as the fortuneteller had told her; but, alas, he had another wife there. He got immediate possession of Sally's £20. Rachel put in for her share, but he refused to give her a farthing, and bade her get away, or he would have her taken up on the vagrant act. He soon ran away from Sally, leaving her to bewail her own weakness; for it was that indeed, and not any irresistible fate, which had been the cause of her ruin. To complete the misery, she herself was suspected of having stolen the silver cup which Rachel had pocketed. Her master, however, would not prosecute her, as she was falling into a deep decline, and she died in a few months of a broken heart, a sad warning to all credulous girls.

Rachel, whenever she got near home, used to drop her trade of fortunetelling, and only dealt in the wares of her basket. Mr. Wilson, the clergyman, found her one day dealing out some very wicked ballads to some children. He went up with a view to give her a reprimand; but had no sooner begun his exhortation than up came a constable, followed by several people.

"There she is, that is she, that is the old witch who tricked my wife out of the five guineas," said one of them. "Do your office, constable; seize the old hag. She may tell fortunes and find pots of gold in Taunton jail, for there she will have nothing else to do."

This was that very farmer Jenkins, whose wife had been cheated by Rachel of the five guineas. He had taken pains to trace her to her own parish: he did not so much value the loss of the money, but he thought it was a duty he owed the public to clear the country of such vermin. Mr. Wilson immediately committed her. She took her trial at the next assizes, when she was sentenced to a year's imprisonment.

In the meantime the pawnbroker to whom she had sold the silver cup, which she had stolen from poor Sally's master, impeached her; and as the robbery was fully proved upon Rachel, she was sentenced for this crime to Botany Bay; and a happy day it was for the county of Somerset, when such a nuisance was sent out of it. She was transported much about the same time that her husband Giles lost his life, in stealing the net from the garden wall, as related in the second part of Poaching Giles.

I have thought it my duty to print this little history, as a kind of warning to all young men and maidens, not to have any thing to say to cheats, impostors, cunning women, fortunetellers, conjurers, and interpreters of dreams. Listen to me, your true friend, when I assure you that God never reveals to weak and wicked women those secret designs of his providence, which no human wisdom is able to foresee. To consult these false oracles is not only foolish, but sinful. It is foolish, because they are themselves as ignorant as those whom they pretend to teach; and it is sinful, because it is prying into that futurity which God, in mercy as well as wisdom, hides from men.

God indeed orders all things; but when you have a mind to do a foolish thing, do not fancy you are fated to do it. This is tempting Providence, and not trusting him. It is, indeed, "charging God with folly." Prudence is his gift, and you obey him better when you make use of prudence under the direction of prayer, than when you madly run into ruin, and think you are only submitting to your fate. Never fancy that you are compelled to undo yourself, or to rush upon your own destruction, in compliance with any supposed fatality. Never believe that God conceals his will from a sober Christian who obeys his laws, and reveals it to a vagabond gypsy, who runs up and down, breaking the laws both of God and man. King Saul never consulted the witch till he had left off serving God. The Bible will direct us what to do, better than any conjurer; and no days are unlucky but those which we make so by our own vanity, folly, and sin.

THE HAPPY WATERMAN

A gentleman and lady walking on the bank of the river Thames, spied a small ferryboat, with a neatlydressed waterman, rowing towards them; on his nearer approach, they read on the stern of his boat these words, THE HAPPY WATERMAN. Without taking any notice of it, they determined to enter into conversation with him; and inquiring into his situation in life, they found that he had a wife and five children, and supported also an old father and motherinlaw by his own labor. The gentleman and lady were upon this still more surprised at the title he had given himself, and said,

"My friend, if this is your situation, how is it that you call yourself 'the happy waterman'?"

"I can easily explain this to your satisfaction," answered the young man, "if you will give me leave;" and they desiring him to proceed, he spoke as follows: "I have observed that the greatest blessings in life are often looked upon as the greatest distresses, and are, in fact, made such by means of imprudent conduct. My father and mother died a few years ago, and left a large family. My father was a waterman, and I was his assistant in the management of a ferryboat, by which he supported his family. On his death, it was necessary, in order to pay his just debts, to sell our boat. I parted from it, even with tears; but the distress that I felt spurred me on to industry, for I said, 'I will use every kind of diligence to purchase my boat back again.' I went to the person who had bought it, and told him my design; he had given five guineas for it, but told me, as I was once the owner, that I should have it whenever I could raise five pounds. 'Shall the boat be mine again?' said I; and my heart bounded at the thought.

"I was at this time married to a good young woman, and we lived at a neighboring cottage; she was young, healthy, and industrious, and so was I, and we loved one another. What might we not undertake? My father used to say to me, 'Always do what is right; labor diligently, and spend your money carefully, and God will bless your store.' We treasured up these rules, and determined to try the truth of them.

"My wife had long chiefly supported two aged parents: I loved them as my own; and the desire of contributing to their support was an additional spur to my endeavors to repurchase the boat. I entered myself as a daylaborer in the garden of our squire; and my wife was called occasionally to perform some services at the house, and employed herself in needlework, spinning, or knitting at home. Not a moment in the day was suffered to pass unemployed. We spared for ourselves, and furnished all the comforts we could to the poor about us; and every week we dropped a little overplus into a fairingbox, to buy the boat. If any accident of charity brought us an additional shilling, we did not enlarge our expense, but kept it for the boat. The more care we took, the more comfortable we felt, for we were the nearer the possession of our little boat. Our labor was lightened by looking forward to the attainment of our wishes.

"Our family indeed increased, but with it our friends increased also; for the cleanliness and frugality which furnished our cottage, and the content and cheerfulness that appeared in it, drew the notice of our rich neighborsof my master and mistress particularly, whose rule was to assist the industrious, but not to encourage the idle. They did not approve of giving money to the poor, but in cold winters, or dear times, allowed us to buy things at a cheaper rate; this was money to us, for when we counted our little cash for the week's marketing, all that was saved to us by our tickets to purchase things at reduced prices, went into our 'little box.' If my children got a penny at school for a reward to buy gingerbread, they brought it home, they said, to help me to buy the boatfor they would have no gingerbread till father had got his boat again. Thus, from time to time, our little store insensibly increased, till one pound only was wanting of the five, when the following accident happened.

"Coming home one evening from my work, I saw in the road a small pocketbook: on opening it, I found a banknote of ten pounds, which plainly enough belonged to my master, for his name was upon it, and I had also seen him passing that way in the evening: it being too late, however, to return to the house, I went on my way. When I told my family of the incident, the little ones were thrown into a transport of joy.

"'My dears,' said I, 'what is the matter?'

"'Oh, father, the BOAT! the BOAT! we may now have two or three boats!'

"I checked them by my looks, and asked them if they recollected whose money that was. They said, 'Yours, as you found it.' I reminded them that I was not the real owner, and bade them think how they would all feel, supposing a stranger was to take our box of money, if I should happen to drop it on the day I went to buy back the boat."

"This thought had the effect on their young minds that I desired; they were silent and pale with the representation of such a disaster, and I begged it might be a lesson to them never to forget the golden rule of 'doing as they would wish others to do by them;' for by attention to this certain guide, no one would ever do wrong to another. I also took this opportunity to explain to them, that the possession of the boat by dishonest means would never answer, since we could not expect the blessing of God upon bad deeds."

"To go on with my story: The next morning I put the pocketbook into my bosom, and went to my work, intending, as soon as the family rose, to give it to my master; but what were my feelings when, on searching in my bosom, it was nowhere to be found! I hasted back along the road by which I came, and looked diligently all the way, but in vain; there was no trace of any such thing. I would not return into my cottage, because I wished to save my family the pain I felt; and in the hope of still recovering the book, I went to my work, following another path which I recollected I had also gone by. On my return to the gardengate, I was accosted by the gardener, who, in a threatening tone, told me I was suspected; that our master had lost a pocketbook, describing what I had found, and that I being the only man absent from the garden at the hour of work, the rest of the men also denying that they had seen any such thing, there was every reason to conclude that I must have got it.

"Before I could answer, my distressed countenance confirmed the suspicion; and another servant coming up, said I was detected, for that a person had been sent to my house, and that my wife and family had owned it all, and had described the pocketbook. I told them the real fact, but it seemed to every one unlikely to be true; every circumstance was against me, andmy heart trembles to look back upon itI was arrested, and hurried away to prison. I protested my innocence, but I did not wonder that I gained no credit.

"Great grief now oppressed my heart; my poor wife, my dear children, and my greyheaded parents, were all at once plunged into want and misery, instead of the ease and happiness which we were expecting; for we were just arriving at the height of our earthly wishes. I had, however, one consolation leftthat I knew I was innocent; and I trusted that by persevering in honesty, all might come right at last. My resolution was, as I had certainly been the cause, though without any design, of the second loss of the property, that I would offer the whole of our little store, to make it good as far as in my power; and I sent for my wife to give her this sad commission, but she informed me that even this sacrifice could be of no avail; 'for,' said she, 'my master has been at the cottage, when I told him freely how you had found the note, but, unfortunately, had lost it again; and I added, that I was sure both I and my husband would make the best return in our power; after which I produced our little fairingbox, and begged him to accept the contents, which had been so long raising, as all we had to offer.' But, sir," said the waterman, "conceive my agony, when she added, that my master angrily refused, saying, that our being in possession of all that money was of itself the clearest proof of my guilt; for it was impossible, with my large family, and no greater opportunities than my neighbors, that I could come honestly by such a sum; therefore he was determined to keep me in jail till I should pay the whole.

"My unhappiness was very great; however, my mind by degrees began to be more easy, for I grew confident that I should not trust in God and my own innocence in vainand so it happened: one of my fellowlaborers proved to be the person who had picked up the note after I had dropped it, having come a few minutes after me along the same road to his work, and hearing that the suspicion had fallen altogether upon me, he was tempted to turn the accident to his own advantage, and conceal the property; which having kept in his own box for a few weeks, till he thought no suspicion would rest upon him, he went and offered the note for change, and being then suspected, my master had him taken up, and I was released.

"The second change, from so much misery to happiness, was almost too much for us. My master sent for me, and with many expressions of concern for what had passed, made me give him an account of the means by which I had collected the little fund that fixed his suspicions so strongly upon me. I accordingly related the history of it as I have now done; and when I came to that part where I checked my children for their inconsiderate joy on finding the note, he rose with much kindness in his looks, and putting the bankbill into my hand, he said,

"'Take it; the banknote shall be theirs. It is the best and only return I can make you, as well as a just reward of your honesty; and it will be a substantial proof to your children of the goodness of your instructions, for they will thus early see and feel the benefit of honesty and virtue.'

"This kind and worthy gentleman interested himself much in the purchase of my boat, which, in less than a week, I was in full possession of. The remainder of my master's bounty, and the additional advantage of the ferry, has placed me in comfortable circumstances, which I humbly trust God will continue to us as long as we continue our labor and honest diligence; and I can say from my long experience, that the fruit of our own industry is always sweetest. I have now also the pleasure of being able to help others; for when a rich passenger takes my ferry, as my story is well known in the neighborhood, he often gives me more than my fare, which enables me to let the next poor person go over for half price."

The lady and gentleman were extremely pleased with the waterman's story, and willingly joined in calling him the happy waterman. They passed over in his ferryboat for the sake of making him a handsome present. And from this time becoming acquainted with his family, they did them every service in their power, giving books and schooling to the little ones, and every comfort to the old father and motherinlaw as long as they survived. They were very desirous of knowing what became of the unfortunate fellowlaborer, who had so dreadfully gone aside from the principles of honesty, and they learned that he was, after a short imprisonment, set at liberty by his master at the earnest entreaty of the honest waterman, as he said it was partly through his carelessness in losing the note, that the temptation had fallen in his fellowlaborer's way; he had, moreover, a very large family. His master also was so good as to consider that he was a man who had not been blessed with a good education in his youth; so that having little fear of God before his eyes, and having a great temptation in his way, he had been the more easily led to commit this very wicked action, by which he would have enriched himself at the expense of an innocent man.

I have great pleasure in adding, that the thought of what he had done, together with the generosity of the waterman, had so strong an effect upon this poor fellow, that he afterwards had it written upon his cottage door, DO AS YOU WOULD BE DONE UNTO. And he has resolved to follow this rule himself in future, and also taught it to all his children. Indeed, it became a rule well known over the whole parish; for every little child having been informed of this story, was told that he ought to consider, before he did any action, whether he would like his brother, or sister, or schoolfellow to do the same by him; and if not, that the action was wrong, and not to be done, let the profit be ever so great. Surely, then, those who have lived long, and seen much of life, and have had much religious instruction also, should never depart from this simple and certain rule. And it is the same to all ranksit requires neither learning nor abilities to "do as you would be done unto;" nor can any station, however great, no, nor any circumstances, however trying, excuse men from giving their constant attention to this golden rule.

THE GRAVESTONE.

Here rests in peace a Christian wife,
Safe from the cares and ills of life;
Taught by kind Heaven's afflicting rod,
She well had learned her way to GOD.
Once a gay girl, she trod the green,
The foremost in the festive scene;
'Twas then she followed all her will,
And wedded William of the hill.
No heart had he for prayer and praise,
No thought of God's most holy ways:
Of worldly gains he loved to speak,
In worldly cares he spent his week;
E'en Sunday passed unheeded by,
And both forgot that they must die.
While thus by Satan quite beguiled,
The God of mercy smote her child:
Bereft of one sweet infant dear,
She shed the mother's mournful tear;
A second next she tried to save,
Then bore the second to the grave;
Both on one day the parent led
To silent mansions of the dead.
There, while she wept her children's fate.
She learned to feel her mortal state;
Stood pondering all her errors past,
As if that day had been her last;
And as she held the mournful bier,
Dropt for herself a secret tear.
Once she believed her sins were few,
But this one moment cleared her view;
Then first she felt a Saviour's need,
Sinner in thought, and word, and deed.
Of her own worth she ceased to dream,
For Christ's redemption was her theme.
Henceforth her ways were ordered right,
She "walked by faith, and not by sight;"
She read God's word, believed it true,
And strove to practise what she knew.
Her husband saw the mighty change,

And thought at first her humor strange;
Deemed his own worldly ways the best
But soon his error stood confessed.
Ceased is the noise, the jarring strife,
For now how humble is the wife!
He proudly feels each cross event,
While she, poor sinner, is content;
No more she has her stubborn will,
Returns him daily good for ill;
And though her love is still the same.
She loves him with a purer flame.
Oft would she pray the God of grace
His lofty spirit to abase;
Upward his grovelling thoughts to raise,
And teach him humble prayer and praise.
Heaven heard her voice: the youth so gay,
The thoughtless sinner, learned to pray;
Sad sickness too, with pain and smart,
Was sent to soften all his heart.
She followed next her husband's bier,
She wiped his last repenting tear;
She heard him mourn his former pride,
She heard him thank her when he died.
Here, then, in hope of endless life,
Rest both the husband and the wife;
Here too, the babes whom God hath given,
And such, we trust, shall enter heaven.

ADDRESS TO PERSONS ATTENDING A FUNERAL.

Ye mourners, who in silent gloom
Bear your dear kindred to the tomb,
Grudge not, when Christians go to rest;
They sleep in JESUS, and are blest.
Call then to mind their faith, their love,
Their meetness for the realms above;
And if to heaven a saint is fled,
O mourn the living, not the dead;
Weep o'er the thousands that remain,
Deep sunk in sin, or racked with pain;
Mourn your own crimes and wicked ways,
And learn to number all your days;
Gain wisdom from this mournful stone,
And make this Christian's case your own.

PARLEY THE PORTER.

AN ALLEGORY.
SHOWING HOW ROBBERS WITHOUT
CAN NEVER GET INTO A HOUSE
UNLESS THERE ARE TRAITORS WITHIN.

BY HANNAH MORE.

There was once a certain gentleman who had a house, or castle, situated in the midst of a great wilderness, but inclosed in a garden. Now there was a band of robbers in the wilderness, who had a great mind to plunder and destroy the castle; but they had not succeeded in their endeavors, because the master had given strict orders to "watch without ceasing." To quicken their vigilance, he used to tell them that their care would soon have an end; that though the nights they had to watch were dark and stormy, yet they were but few; the period of resistance Was shortthat of rest would be eternal.

The robbers, however, attacked the castle in various ways. They tried at every avenue; watched to take advantage of every careless moment; looked for an open door, or a neglected window. But though they often made the bolts shake and the windows rattle, they could never greatly hurt the house, much less get into it. Do you know the reason? It was, because the servants were never off their guard. They heard the noises plain enough, and used to be not a little frightened, for they were aware both of the strength and perseverance of their enemies. But what seemed rather odd to some of these servants, the gentleman used to tell them, that while they continued to be afraid, they would be safe; and it passed into a sort of proverb in that family, "Happy is he that feareth always." Some of the servants however, thought this a contradiction.

One day when the master was going from home, he called his servants all together, and spoke to them as follows: "I will not repeat to you the directions I have so often given you; they are all written down in the book of laws, of which every one of you has a copy. Remember, it is a very short time that you are to remain in this castle; you will soon remove to my more settled habitation, to a more durable house, not made with hands. As that house is never exposed to any attack, so it never stands in need of any repair; for that country is never infested by any sons of violence. Here, you are servants; there, you will be princes.

"But mark my words, and you will find the same truth in the book of my laws: Whether you will ever attain to that house, will depend on the manner in which you defend yourselves in this. A stout vigilance for a short time will secure your certain happiness for ever. But every thing depends on your present exertions. Don't complain and take advantage of my absence, and call me a hard master, and grumble that you are placed in the midst of a howling wilderness, without peace or security. Say not, that you are exposed to temptations without any power to resist them. You have some difficulties, it is true; but you have many helps and many comforts to make this house tolerable, even before you get to the other. Yours is not a hard service; and if it were, 'the time is short.' You have arms if you will use them, and doors if you will bar them, and strength if you will use it. I would defy all the attacks of the robbers without, if I could depend on the fidelity of the people within. If the thieves ever get in and destroy the house, it must be by the connivance of one of the family. For it is a standing law of this castle, that mere outward attack can never destroy it, if there be no traitor within. You will stand or fall as you observe this rule. If you are finally happy, it will be by my grace and favor; if you are ruined, it will be your own fault."

"When the gentleman had done speaking, every servant repeated his assurance of attachment and firm allegiance to his master. But among them all, not one was so vehement and loud in his professions as old Parley the porter. Parley, indeed, it was well known, was always talking, which exposed him to no small danger; for as he was the foremost to promise, so he was the slackest to perform. And, to speak the truth, though he was a civilspoken fellow, his master was more afraid of him, with all his professions, than he was of the rest, who protested less. He knew that Parley was vain, credulous, and selfsufficient; and he always apprehended more danger from Parley's impertinence, curiosity, and love of novelty, than even from the stronger vices of some of the other servants. The rest, indeed, seldom got into any scrape of which Parley was not the cause, in some shape or other."

I am sorry to be obliged to confess, that though Parley was allowed every refreshment, and all the needful rest which the nature of his place permitted, yet he thought it very hard to be forced to be so constantly on duty.

"Nothing but watching," said Parley; "I have, to be sure, many pleasures, and meat sufficient; and plenty of chat in virtue of my office; and I pick up a good deal of news of the comers and goers by day; but it is hard that at night I must watch as narrowly as a housedog, and yet let in no company without orders, only because there are said to be a few straggling robbers here in the wilderness, with whom my master does not care to let us be acquainted. He pretends to make us vigilant through fear of the robbers, but I suspect it is only to make us mope alone. A merry companion, and a mug of beer, would make the night pass cheerfully."

Parley, however, kept all these thoughts to himself, or uttered them only when no one heardfor talk he must. He began to listen to the nightly whistling of the robbers under the windows with rather less alarm than formerly; and he was sometimes so tired of watching, that he thought it was even better to run the risk of being robbed once, than to live always in fear of robbers.

There were certain bounds in which the gentleman allowed his servants to walk and divert themselves at all proper seasons. A pleasant garden surrounded the castle, and a thick hedge separated it from the wilderness, which was infested by the robbers. In this garden they were permitted to amuse themselves. The master advised them always to keep within these bounds. "While you observe this rule," said he, "you will be safe and well; and you will consult your own safety, as well as show your love to me, by not venturing even to the extremity of your bounds. He who goes as far as he dares, always shows a wish to go farther than he ought, and commonly does so."

It was remarkable, that the nearer these servants kept to the castle, and the farther from the hedge, the more ugly the wilderness appeared. And the nearer they approached the forbidden bounds, their own home appeared more dull, and the wilderness more delightful. And this the master knew when he gave his orders, for he never either did or said any thing without a good reason. And when his servants sometimes desired an explanation of the reason, he used to tell them they would understand it when they came to the other house; for it was one of the pleasures of that house, that it would explain all the mysteries of this, and any little obscurities in the master's conduct would be then made quite plain.

Parley was the first who promised to keep clear of the hedge, and yet was often seen looking as near as he durst. One day he ventured close up to the hedge, put two or three stones one on another, and tried to peep over. He saw one of the robbers strolling as near as could be on the forbidden side. This man's name was Flatterwell, a smooth, civil man, "whose words were softer than butter, having war in his heart." He made several low bows to Parley.

Now Parley knew so little of the world, that he actually concluded all robbers must have an ugly look, which should frighten you at once; and coarse, brutal manners, which would, at first sight, show they were enemies. He thought, like a poor ignorant fellow as he was, that this mild, specious person could never be one of the band. Flatterwell accosted Parley with the utmost civility, which put him quite off his guard; for Parley had no notion that he could be an enemy who was so soft and civil. For an open foe he would have been prepared. Parley, however, after a little discourse, drew this conclusion, that either Mr. Flatterwell could not be one of the gang, or if he was, the robbers themselves could not be such monsters as his master had described, and therefore it was a folly to be afraid of them.

Flatterwell began, like a true adept in his art, by lulling all Parley's suspicions asleep, and instead of openly abusing his master, which would have opened Parley's eyes at once, he pretended rather to commend him in a general way, as a person who meant well himself, but was too apt to suspect others. To this Parley assented. The other then ventured to hint by degrees, that though the gentleman might be a good master in the main, yet he must say he was a little strict, and a little stingy, and not a little censorious. That he was blamed by the gentlemen in the wilderness for shutting his house against good company, and his servants were laughed at by people of spirit for submitting to the gloomy life of the castle, and the insipid pleasures of the garden, instead of ranging in the wilderness at large.

"It is true enough," said Parley, who was generally of the opinion of the person he was talking with; "my master is rather harsh and close. But, to own the truth, all the barring, and locking, and bolting, is to keep out a set of gentlemen who he assures us are robbers, and who are waiting for an opportunity to destroy us. I hope no offence, sir, but by your livery I suspect you, sir, are one of the gang he is so much afraid of."

FLATTERWELL. "Afraid of me! impossible, dear Mr. Parley. You see I do not look like an enemy. I am unarmed; what harm can a plain man like me do?"

PARLEY. "Why, that is true enough. Yet my master says, that if we were once to let you into the house, we should be ruined, soul and body."

FLATTERWELL. "I am sorry, Mr. Parley, that so sensible a man as you are so deceived. This is mere prejudice. He knows we are cheerful, entertaining people; foes to gloom and superstition; and therefore, he is so morose, he will not let you get acquainted with us."

PARLEY. "Well, he says you are a band of thieves, gamblers, murderers, drunkards, and atheists."

FLATTERWELL. "Don't believe him: the worst we should do, perhaps, is, we might drink a friendly glass with you to your master's health, or play an innocent game at cards just to keep you awake, or sing a cheerful song with the maids; now is there any harm in all this?"

PARLEY. "Not the least in the world. And I begin to think there is not a word of truth in all my master says."

FLATTERWELL. "The more you know us, the more you will like us. But I wish there was not this ugly hedge between us. I have a great deal to say, and I am afraid of being overheard."

Parley was now just going to give a spring over the hedge, but checked himself, saying, "I dare not come on your side; there are people about, and every thing is carried to my master."

Flatterwell saw by this that his new friend was kept on his own side of the hedge by fear rather than by principle, and from that moment he made sure of him. "Dear Mr. Parley," said he, "if you will allow me the honor of a little conversation with you, I will call under the window of your lodge this evening. I have something to tell you greatly to your advantage. I admire you exceedingly. I long for your friendship; our whole brotherhood is ambitious of being known to so amiable a person."

"O dear," said Parley, "I shall be afraid of talking to you at night; it is so against my master's orders. But did you say you had something to tell me to my advantage?"

"Yes," replied Flatterwell, "I can point out to you how you may be a richer, a merrier, and a happier man. If you will admit me tonight under the window, I will convince you that 'tis prejudice, and not wisdom, which makes your master bar his door against us; I will convince you, that the mischief of a 'robber,' as your master scurrilously calls us, is only in the namethat we are your true friends, and only mean to promote your happiness."

"Don't say we," said Parley, "pray come alone, I would not see the rest of the gang for the world; but I think there can be no great harm in talking to you through the bars, if you come alone; but I am determined not to let you in. Yet I can't say but I wish to know what you can tell me so much to my advantage; indeed, if it is for my good, I ought to know it."

"Dear Mr. Parley," said Flatterwell, (going out, but turning back,) "there is one thing I had forgot, I cannot get over the hedge at night without assistance. You know there is a secret in the nature of that hedge: you in the house may get over to us in the wilderness of your own accord, but we cannot get to your side by our own strength. You must look about and see where the hedge is thinnest, and then set to work to clear away here and there a little bough for me; it wont be missed: and if there is but the smallest hole made on your side, those on ours can get through; otherwise, we do but labor in vain."

To this Parley made some objection through the fear of being seen. Flatterwell replied, that "the smallest hole from within would be sufficient, for he could then work his own way."

"Well," said Parley, "I will consider of it. To be sure, I shall even then be equally safe in the castle, as I shall have all the bolts, bars, and locks between us; so it will make but little difference."

"Certainly not," said Flatterwell, who knew it would make all the difference in the world. So they parted with mutual protestations of regard. Parley went home charmed with his new friend. His eyes were now clearly open as to his master's prejudices against the "robbers," and he was convinced there was more in the name than in the thing.

"But," said he, "though Mr. Flatterwell is certainly an agreeable companion, he may not be so safe an inmate. There can, however, be no harm in talking at a distance, and I certainly wont let him in."

Parley, in the course of the day, did not forget his promise to thin the hedge of separation a little. At first he only tore off a handful of leaves, then a little sprig, then he broke away a bough or two. It was observable, the larger the breach became, the worse he began to think of his master, and the better of himself. Every peep he took through the broken hedge increased his desire to get out into the wilderness, and made the thoughts of the castle more irksome to him.

He was continually repeating to himself, "I wonder what Mr. Flatterwell can have to say so much to my advantage? I see he does not wish to hurt my master, he only wishes to serve me." As the hour of meeting, however, drew near, the master's orders now and then came across Parley's thoughts; so, to divert them, he took the book. He happened to open it at these words: "My son, if sinners entice thee, consent thou not." For a moment his heart failed him. "If this admonition should be sent on purpose," said he; "but no, 'tis a bugbear. My master told me that if I went to the bounds, I should get over the hedge. Now I went to the utmost limits, and did not get over." Here conscience put in, "Yes, but it was because you were watched." "I am sure," continued Parley, "one may always stop where one will, and this is only a trick of my master's to spoil sport; so I will even hear what Mr. Flatterwell has to say so much to my advantage. I am not obliged to follow his counsels, but there can be no harm in hearing them."

Flatterwell prevailed on the rest of the robbers to make no public attack on the castle that night. "My brethren," said he, "you now and then fail in your schemes, because you are for violent beginnings; while my soothing, insinuating measures hardly ever miss.

You come blustering and roaring, and frighten people, and set them on their guard. You inspire them with terror of you, while my whole scheme is to make them think well of themselves, and ill of their master. If I once get them to entertain hard thoughts of him, and high thoughts of themselves, my business is done, and they fall plump into my snares. So, let this delicate affair alone to me. Parley is a softly fellow: he must not be frightened, but cajoled. He is the very sort of man to succeed with, and worth a hundred of your sturdy, sensible fellows. With them we want strong arguments and strong temptations; but with such fellows as Parley, in whom vanity and sensuality are the leading qualitiesas, let me tell you, is the case with far the greater partflattery, and a promise of ease and pleasure, will do more than your whole battle array. If you will let me manage, I will get you all into the castle before midnight."

At night the castle was barricaded as usual, and no one had observed the hole which Parley had made in the hedge. This oversight arose that night from the servants neglecting one of the master's standing ordersto make a nightly examination of the state of the castle. The neglect did not proceed so much from wilful disobedience, as from having passed the evening in sloth and diversion, which often amounts to nearly the same in its consequences.

As all was very cheerful within, so all was very quiet without. And before they went to bed some of the servants observed to the rest, that as they heard no robbers that night, they thought they might soon begin to remit something of their diligence in bolting and barring. That all this fastening and looking was very troublesome, and they hoped the danger was now pretty well over. It was rather remarkable, that they never made this sort of observations, but after an evening of some excess, and when they had neglected their private business with their master. All, however, except Parley, went quietly to bed, and seemed to feel uncommon security.

Parley crept down to his lodge. He had half a mind to go to bed too. Yet he was not willing to disappoint Mr. Flatterwell; so civil a gentleman. To be sure, he might have bad designs. Yet what right had he to suspect any body who made such professions, and who was so very civil. "Besides, it is something for my advantage," added Parley. "I will not open the door, that is certain; but as he is to come alone, he can do me no harm through the bars of the windows. And he will think I am a coward, if I don't keep my word; no, I will let him see that I am not afraid of my own strength; I will show him I can go what length I please, and stop short when I please." Had Flatterwell heard this boastful speech, he would have been quite sure of his man.

About eleven Parley heard the signal agreed upon. It was so gentle as to cause little alarm. So much the worse. Flatterwell never frightened any one, and therefore seldom failed of any one. Parley stole softly down, planted himself at his little window, opened the casement, and spied his new friend. It was pale starlight. Parley was a little frightened, for he thought he perceived one or two persons behind Flatterwell; but the other assured him it was only his own shadow, which his fears had magnified into a company. "Though I assure you," said he, "I have not a friend but what is as harmless as myself."

They now entered into earnest discourse, in which Flatterwell showed himself a deep politician. He skilfully mixed up in his conversation a proper proportion of praise on the pleasures of the wilderness, of compliments to Parley, of ridicule on his master, and of abusive sneers on the book in which the master's laws were written. Against this last he had always a particular spite, for he considered it as the grand instrument by which the master maintained his servants in allegiance; and when they could be once brought to sneer at the book, there was an end of submission to the master. Parley had not penetration enough to see his drift. "As to the book, Mr. Flatterwell," said he, "I do not know whether it be true or false; I rather neglect than disbelieve it. I am forced, indeed, to hear it read once a week; but I never look into it myself, if I can help it." "Excellent," said Flatterwell to himself; "that is just the same thing. This is safe ground for me. For whether a man does not believe in the book, or does not attend to it, it comes pretty much to the same, and I generally get him at last."

"Why cannot we be a little nearer, Mr. Parley?" said Flatterwell; "I am afraid of being overheard by some of your master's spies, the window from which you speak is so high. I wish you would come down to the door."

"Well," said Parley, "I see no great harm in that. There is a little wicket in the door, through which we can converse with more ease and equal safety. The same fastenings will be still between us." So down he went, but not without a degree of fear and trembling.

The little wicket being now opened, and Flatterwell standing close on the outside of the door, they conversed with great ease. "Mr. Parley," said Flatterwell, "I should not have pressed you so much to admit me into the castle, but out of pure, disinterested regard to your own happiness. I shall get nothing by it, but I cannot bear to think that a person so wise and amiable should be shut up in this gloomy dungeon, under a hard master, and a slave to the unreasonable tyranny of his book of laws. If you admit me, you need have no more waking, no more watching."

Here Parley involuntarily slipped back the bolt of the door.

"To convince you of my true love," continued Flatterwell, "I have brought a bottle of the most delicious wine that grows in the wilderness. You shall taste it; but you must put a glass through the wicket to receive it; for it is a singular property in this wine, that we of the wilderness cannot succeed in conveying it to you of the castle, without you hold out a vessel to receive it."

"O here is a glass," said Parley, holding out a large goblet, which he always kept ready to be filled by any chance comer.

The other immediately poured into the capacious goblet a large draught of that delicious intoxicating liquor with which the family of the Flatterwells have, for near six thousand years, gained the hearts and destroyed the souls of all the inhabitants of the castle, whenever they have been able to prevail on them to hold out a hand to receive it. This the wise master of the castle well knew would be the case, for he knew what was in menhe knew their propensity to receive the delicious poison of the Flatterwells; and it was for this reason that he gave them the book of his laws, and planted the hedge, and invented the bolts, and doubled the locks.

As soon as poor Parley had swallowed the fatal draught it acted like enchantment. He at once lost all power of resistance. He had no sense of fear left. He despised his own safety, forgot his master, lost all sight of the house in the other country, and reached out for another draught as eagerly as Flatterwell held out the bottle to administer it. "What a fool have I been," said Parley, "to deny myself so long."

"Will you now let me in?" said Flatterwell.

"Aye, that I will," said the deluded Parley. Though the train was now increased to near a hundred robbers, yet so intoxicated was Parley, that he did not see one of them, except his new friend. Parley eagerly pulled down the bars, drew back the bolts, and forced open the locks, thinking he could never let in his friend soon enough. He had, however, just presence of mind to say, "My dear friend, I hope you are alone." Flatterwell swore he was. Parley opened the doorin rushed, not Flatterwell only, but the whole banditti, who always lurk behind in his train. The moment they had got sure possession, Flatterwell changed his soft tone, and cried out in a voice of thunder, "Down with the castle; kill, burn, and destroy."

Rapine, murder, and conflagration by turns took place. Parley was the very first whom they attacked. He was overpowered with wounds. As he fell, he cried out, "O my master, I die a victim to my unbelief in thee, and to my own vanity and imprudence. O that the guardians of all other castles would hear me with my dying breath repeat my master's admonition, that all attacks from without will not destroy, unless there is some confederate within. O that the keepers of all other castles would learn from my ruin, that he who parleys with temptation is already undone. That he who allows himself to go to the very bounds, will soon jump over the hedge; that he who talks out of the window with the enemy, will soon open the door to him; that he who holds out his hand for the cup of sinful flattery, loses all power of resisting; that when he opens the door to one sin, all the rest fly in upon him, and the man perishes as I now do."

A NEW CHRISTMAS TRACT;

OR,
THE RIGHT WAY OF REJOICING AT CHRISTMAS,
SHOWING THE REASONS WE HAVE FOR JOY
AT THE EVENT OF OUR SAVIOUR'S BIRTH.

There are two ways of keeping Christmas: some seem to keep it much in the same way in which the unbelieving Jews kept their feast in honor of the calf which they had made. "And they made a calf in Horeb in those days, and the people sat down to eat and drink, and rose up to play." But what a sad sort of Christianity is this! I am no enemy to mirth of a proper kind, and at proper seasons; but the mirth I now speak of, is the mirth of inconsideration and folly, and is often mixed with much looseness of conduct and drunkenness. Is this, then, the sort of mirth proper for Christians? Let us suppose, now, that a man should choose a church as the place in which he was to sit and sing his jolly song, and to drink till he was intoxicated; surely this would imply that he was a person of extraordinary wickedness. But this, you will say, is what nobody is so bad as to be guilty of; well, then, let us suppose, that instead of choosing a church as the place, he should choose Christmas as the time for the like acts of riot and drunkenness: methinks this must imply no small degree of the same kind of wickedness; for, as he that should get intoxicated in a church, would insult the church, so he that gets intoxicated at Christmas, which is the season for commemorating the birth of Christ, insults Christ and his religion.

I know it may be said, that those who take these liberties at Christmas do not mean to insult Christ, and that they act from inconsideration: to which I answer, that they are very guilty in being so inconsiderate; for I would just remark by the way, that these people who are so very inconsiderate in some things, are apt to be very considerate in others. For instance, they are very considerate about their pleasures, but very inconsiderate about their duty. They are often, perhaps, very considerate about this world, always very inconsiderate about eternity; very considerate for themselves, and very little so about other people; extremely considerate on their own side of a bargain, but as inconsiderate about the side of the other party; and when they have committed a sin, they are apt to be very considerate in finding excuses for it, but very inconsiderate in tracing out the guilt and mischief of their wickedness. In short, then, let it be remembered, that inconsideration is often neither more nor less than another word for wickedness, and that the inconsiderate way of spending Christmas which has been spoken of, is only, in other words, the wicked way of spending it.

But now let us come to the true way of keeping it.

First, then, in order to know how the time of Christ's birth ought to be remembered by us, I would observe, that it is necessary to understand well who Christ was, and for what purpose he came on earth. How absurd would it be to celebrate the fifth of November, without knowing, that on that day the houses of parliament were saved from fire, and our happy constitution, as well as our religion, was preserved to us. Again, how absurd would it be for any man to celebrate the king's birthday, or coronationday, who did not feel within his heart loyalty and affection towards his sovereign, and who did not think that any blessings were derived from our kingly government.

Let every one, therefore, who wishes to spend Christmas aright, get acquainted with the benefits which have followed from Christ's coming into the world. We will endeavor, now, to show very briefly what these benefits have been. The world, at the time of Christ's appearing, was divided into Jews and Gentiles. The word Gentiles signifies nations, that is, all the nations except the Jews. Let us speak of the Gentiles first, and of the Jews afterwards.

The Gentiles were worshippers of false gods; some of one kind, some of another. They all, however, agreed in this, that they thought one god as good as another, and no one among them had any anxiety to bring his neighbor over to his religion, which is a plain proof that they had no true religion among them; for whoever is possessed of true religion, is possessed of a great comfort and blessing, which he will therefore be glad to convey to other people also. It was the custom of some of these Gentiles to worship stocks and stones; others bowed down to living animals, such as bulls, or goats, or lizards; and others paid their stupid adoration to the sun, instead of the Author of it. Many of them worshipped their deceased fellowcreatures; and the dead men who were thus turned into gods had been, in general, some of the most wicked and abominable of the human race.

Now this ignorance of the true God was followedas all ignorance of him is apt to beby great wickedness in their practice. They were "given over" on this account, as St. Paul, the inspired apostle, declares, "to a reprobate mind; to work all uncleanness with greediness." They learned to confound good and evil; vices were then commonly practised, such as are not named among Christians. False principles and false maxims of every kind abounded. Slavery prevailed, even in the most civilized lands; for almost all servants were slaves in those days. The earth was filled with violence. He that had killed the greatest number of his fellowcreatures got usually the greatest praise. "Wars were carried on with dreadful ferocity, and multitudes were massacred at the public games, in battles fought for the amusement of the people. Humanity, kindness, and benevolence, were made of no account; and such a thing as a hospital was not known. Revenge was both practised and recommended; and those excellent Christian graces, humility, universal charity, and forgiveness of injuries, were considered as weaknesses and faults."

I shudder to think of the dreadful state of mankind in those days. God grant that the same evils may never return. They are the natural consequences of being without Christianity in the world; for when Christianity is gone, there is no rule to go by. Every man may then set up a false goodness of his own. Morals, of course, grow worse and worse; a fierce and proud spirit comes in the place of Christian meekness and benevolence, and claims the name of virtue; and the Saviour of the world, with all his works of mercy, being forgotten, man becomes cruel, and unjust, and selfish, and implacable, and unmerciful; for all the violent passions of our nature are let loose.

If we inquire also into the character of the Jews who lived before the coming of our Saviour, we shall find them to have been deplorably corrupt, though they expected his coming, and were, in some measure, acquainted with true religion. The little knowledge which they had seems to have been perverted through the wickedness of their hearts; and the Scriptures assure us, that "both Jews and Gentiles were all under sin." Such was the state into which the world was sunk before the time of our Saviour's appearance in it.

Let us describe, next, who Christ was, and what were the consequences of his coming. He is called in Scripture, "the Son of God;" and in some places, "God's only Son;" which shows that there is no other being like unto him. We know that a son, by his very birth, derives privileges from his father which belong to no other person; that he partakes of the same rank and inheritance with his father; and that he possesses also, in an especial manner, his father's favor, and altogether differs from a stranger or a servant. Christ, then, is to be considered, in all such senses as these, as the Son of God. It is true, he is called also the Son of man, for he was born of a woman, namely, of the virgin Mary, and he took upon him our nature, dwelling on earth for thirty years. We should take great care, however, that his appearance among us as a man, does not lead us to form any low and unworthy notions of him.

Suppose, now, that the son of a king was to travel, in the dress of a private subject, on some merciful and condescending errand to a distant and obscure part of his territory. Surely it would be very ungenerous and ungrateful, if the poor villagers, whom he came to serve, were to deny to him the honors of a king's son merely because they could not believe that so great a person could stoop so low as to come among them, especially if he brought proofs of his power and greatness along with him.

Just so, methinks, are all those persons ungenerous and ungrateful who refuse to Christ that divine honor which belongs to him, merely because he condescended to be made flesh and blood, and to dwell among us. Let us, then, receive with simplicity and humility the scripture testimony concerning him. It speaks of him in terms that are quite astonishing. "His name," says the prophet, foretelling his birth, "shall be called Wonderful, Counsellor, the mighty God, the everlasting Father, the Prince of Peace; and the government shall be on his shoulders." The evangelist John tells us, that "the Word," meaning Christ, "was with God", and the "Word was God." "By him," it is said in the Hebrews, "God made the world;" and again, "Let all the angels of God worship him." "All power hath been given him, both in heaven and earth," and God "hath committed all judgment to the Son." "The hour also cometh when they that are in the graves shall hear the voice of the Son of man, and shall come forth: they that have done good, to the resurrection of life; and they that have done evil, to the resurrection of damnation."

Such are a few of the expressions used in Scripture concerning Christ. Let us learn from these to adore his divine Majesty, and trust his power, as well as to fear his wrath, and to account him able to fulfil all the purposes of his coming.

But let us next describe what these purposes were. It may be said in general, that "it was for us men, and for our salvation, that he came down from heaven;" or, as the Scripture expresses it, "The Son of man came to seek and to save that which was lost, and to give his life a ransom for many."

The world, as hath already been shown, was sunk in sin, and not in sin only, but in condemnation also. Ever since the fall of our first parent Adam, man had been a sinful creature. But as in Adam all died, even so in Christ were all who would receive him, "to be made alive." Christ, then, was the second Adam: as Adam was the destroyer, so Christ was the restorer of our race. The devil, who is called the Prince of darkness, had, as we are told in Scripture, become the god and the prince of this world. Christ, therefore, came into the world, as a conquerer comes, to recover an empire that was lost, and to bring back the rebels to their obedience and to happiness. He came to overthrow that kingdom of darkness which, through the power of the devil and the corruption of man, had been set up. "For this purpose the Son of God was manifested, that he might destroy the works of the devil." He came "to redeem us from all iniquity, and to purify unto himself a peculiar people, zealous of good works."

But how does Christ fulfil his purpose of delivering us? First, I would observe, that he lived a most holy life, hereby setting us an example that we should tread in his steps. He went about doing good: never was any one so kind and gracious to all who came to him as Jesus Christ. I would here observe also, that he preached the gospel to mankind; he told us what we must believe and do, in order to enter into the kingdom of heaven. Through him also the Holy Spirit of God is granted to us. And, to crown all, he died for us. He was nailed to the cross, and suffered a cruel death for our sakes, bearing the wrath of God in our stead. "Herein is love, not that we loved God, but that he loved us, and sent his Son to be the propitiation for our sins." Christ is that Lamb of God "which has been offered up as a sacrifice," and "which taketh away the sins of the world." Now, then, let us rejoice, and say triumphantly, with the prophet of old, "Unto us a child is born, unto us a son is given." "Behold," said the angels, "I bring you good tidings of great joy; for unto you is born this day, a Saviour, which is Christ the Lord." "Glory to God in the highest, on earth peace, good will towards men."

Oh, how many thousands have had reason to bless the season which we are now commemoratingthe season of the birth of Jesus Christ. The world, it is true, is still wicked, for there are many who do not believe in this Saviour; and there are not a few who think they believe in him, and who do not. Nevertheless, even the world in general has been the better for his coming, for the thick darkness is past, and the true light now shineth. Through Christ's coming, iniquity has been lessened even among unbelievers; for real Christians, though few, have held up to view the nature of true goodness, and even bad men have, in some measure, been constrained to imitate them; they have also grown more ashamed than they otherwise would have been of their vices.

But who can calculate the blessing which Christianity hath been to thousands of true believers? How many lives have been made holy here on earth; how many hearts have been cheered and comforted by it; how many deaths, which would otherwise have been most gloomy, have been rendered joyful and triumphant; and, above all, how many immortal souls have been saved and made happy to all eternity, through faith in this blessed Redeemer. "My sheep," says Christ, "hear my voice, and they follow me, and I give unto them eternal life; and they shall never perish, neither shall any pluck them out of my hand." "I go to prepare a place for them, that where I am there they may be also."

And now, reader, what are your thoughts on the subject of our Saviour's appearance on this earth of ours? If you are a true Christian, your language will be such as the following: "It is through the coming of Christ into the world that I have learned to know myself, and to know the God who made me. I am by nature blind and ignorant; I am also sinful and undone; I am utterly without hope, except through the mercy of my Saviour; and even though I have been born in a Christian land, I can trace back, in my recollection, many proofs of this my natural ignorance and corruption and hardness of heart. I was once like a sheep going astray, but I am now returned to the Shepherd of my soul. I followed the bent of my own foolish will, but the grace of God in Jesus Christ has changed my sinful heart; the knowledge of my corruption has humbled me; the thought of my Saviour's dying for me has stirred up gratitude within me, and that acquaintance with his gospel which I have gained has changed my whole views of life.

"Christ's character delights me: I read the history of his humble birth, his painful death, and his glorious resurrection, as it is recorded in Scripture, with hope and joy, and with holy confidence and trust. How shall I sufficiently bless God for Jesus Christ? Whatever change has been wrought in me, I trace to Christ's coming into the world. If Christ had never come, how corrupt should I be at this moment; how blind, how dark, how ignorant, how different from what, through the grace of God, I now am. How miserable, in comparison of my present happiness. I am engaged, indeed, in a sharp conflict with my sins; but, through my Saviour's help, I hope to gain ground against them. I have, occasionally, doubts and fears; but in general, I feel confident that the promises of God are sure and certain in Christ Jesus; for I know in whom I have believed, and I am persuaded that he is able to keep that soul which I have committed to him till the great day."

A NEW CHRISTMAS HYMN.

O how wondrous is the story
Of our blest Redeemer's birth!
See, the mighty Lord of glory
Leaves his heaven to visit earth.
Hear with transport, every creature,
Hear the gospel's joyful sound:
Christ appears in human nature,
In our sinful world is found!
Comes to pardon our transgression,
Like a cloud our sins to blot;
Comes to his own favored nation,
But his own receive him not.

If the angels who attended
To declare the Saviour's birth,
Who from heaven with songs descended,
To proclaim good will on earth;
If, in pity to our blindness,
They had brought the pardon needed;
Still, Jehovah's wondrous kindness
Had our warmest hopes exceeded!
If some prophet had been sent
With salvation's joyful news,
Who that heard the blest event

Could their warmest love refuse?
But 'twas He to whom in heaven
Hallelujahs never cease;
He, the mighty God, was given
Given to us a Prince of peace.
None but he who did create us,
Could redeem from sin and hell;
None but he could reinstate us
In the rank from which we fell.
Had he come, the glorious stranger,
Decked with all the world calls great
Had he lived in pomp and grandeur,
Crowned with more than royal state
Still, our tongues, with praise o'erflowing,

On such boundless love would dwell
Still, our hearts, with rapture glowing,
Speak what words could never tell.
But what wonder should it raise,
Thus our lowest state to borrow!
O the high mysterious ways
God's own Son a child of sorrow!

'Twas to bring us endless pleasure,
He our suffering nature bore;
'Twas to give us heavenly treasure,
He was willing to be poor.
Come, ye rich, survey the stable
Where your infant Saviour lies;
From your full, o'erflowing table,
Send the hungry good supplies.
Boast not your ennobled stations,
Boast not that you're highly fed;
Jesus, hear it all ye nations,

Had not where to lay his head.
Learn of me, thus cries the Saviour,
If my kingdom you'd inherit:
Sinner, quit your proud behavior;
Learn my meek and lowly spirit.
Come, ye servants, see your station
Free from all reproach and shame;
He who purchased your salvation,
Bore a servant's humble name.
Come, ye poor, some comfort gather,
Faint not in the race you run;
Hard the lot your gracious Father

Gave his dear, his only Son.
Think, that if your humble stations
Less of worldly food bestow,
You escape those strong temptations
Which from wealth and grandeur flow
See, your Saviour is ascended;
See, he looks with pity down:
Trust him, all will soon be mended;

Bear his cross, you'll share his crown.

BEAR YE ONE ANOTHER'S BURDENS;

or, THE VALLEY OF TEARS.
A VISION.

BY HANNAH MORE.

Once upon a time methought I set out upon a long journey, and the place through which I travelled appeared to be a dark valley, which was called the Valley of Tears. It had obtained this name not only on account of the many sorrowful adventures which poor passengers commonly meet with in their journey through it, but also because most of these travellers entered it weeping and crying, and left it in a very great pain and anguish. This vast valley was full of people of all colors, ages, sizes, and descriptions; but whether white, or black, or tawney, all were travelling the same road, or rather, they were taking different little paths which all led to the same common end.

Now it was remarkable, that notwithstanding the different complexions, ages, and tempers of this vast variety of people, yet all resembled each other in this one respect, that each had a burden on his back, which he was destined to carry through the toil and heat of the day, until he should arrive, by a longer or shorter course, at his journey's end. These burdens would in general have made the pilgrimage quite intolerable, had not the Lord of the valley, out of his great compassion for these poor pilgrims, provided, among other things, the following means for their relief.

In their full view, over the entrance of the valley, there were written in great letters the following words:

BEAR YE ONE ANOTHER'S BURDENS.

Now I saw in my vision, that many of the travellers hurried on without stopping to read this inscription; and others, though they had once read it, yet paid little or no attention to it. A third sort thought it good advice for other people, but very seldom applied it to themselves. In short, I saw that too many of these people were of the opinion, that they had burdens enough of their own, and that there was therefore no occasion to take upon them those of others; so each tried to make his own load as light, and his own journey as pleasant as he could, without so much as once casting a thought on a poor overloaded neighbor.

Here, however, I have to make a rather singular remark, by which I shall plainly show the folly of these selfish people. It was so ordered and contrived by the Lord of this valley, that if any one stretched out his hand to lighten a neighbor's burden, in fact he never failed to find that he at that moment also lightened his own. Besides, the obligation to help each other, and the benefit of doing so, were mutual. If a man helped his neighbor, it commonly happened that some other neighbor came, by and by, and helped him in his turn; for there was no such thing as what we call independence in the whole valley. Not one of all these travellers, however stout and strong, could move on comfortably without assistance; for so the Lord of the valley, whose laws were all of them kind and good, had expressly ordained.

I stood still to watch the progress of these poor wayfaring people, who moved slowly on, like so many ticketporters, with burdens of various kinds on their backs, of which some were heavier, and some were lighter; but from a burden of one kind or other, not one traveller was entirely free.

THE WIDOW.

A sorrowful widow, oppressed with the burden of grief for the loss of an affectionate husband, would have been bowed down by her heavy load, had not the surviving children with great alacrity stepped forward and supported her. Their kindness, after a while, so much lightened the load, which threatened at first to be intolerable, that she even went on her way with cheerfulness, and more than repaid their help, by applying the strength she derived from it, to their future assistance.

THE HUSBAND.

I next saw a poor old man tottering under a burden so heavy, that I expected him every moment to sink under it. I peeped into his pack, and saw it was made up of many sad articles: there were poverty, oppression, sickness, debt, and what made by far the heaviest part, undutiful children. I was wondering how it was that he got on even so well as he did, till I spied his wife, a kind, meek, Christian woman, who was doing her utmost to assist him. She quietly got behind, gently laid her shoulder to the burden, and carried a much larger proportion of it than appeared to me when I was at a distance. She not only sustained him by her strength, but cheered him by her counsels. She told him that "through much tribulation we must enter into the kingdom;" that "he that overcometh shall inherit all things." In short, she so supported his fainting spirit, that he was enabled to "run with patience the race that was set before him."

THE KIND NEIGHBOR.

An infirm blind woman was creeping forward with a very heavy burden, in which were packed sickness and want, with numberless other of those raw materials out of which human misery is worked up. She was so weak that she could not have got on at all, had it not been for the kind assistance of another woman almost as poor as herself; who, though she had no light burden of her own, cheerfully lent a helping hand to a fellowtraveller who was still more heavily laden. This friend had indeed little or nothing to give; but the very voice of kindness is soothing to the weary. And I remarked in many other cases, that it was not so much the degree of help afforded as the manner of helping, that lightened the burdens.

Some had a coarse, rough, clumsy way of assisting a neighbor, which, though in fact it might be of real use, yet seemed, by galling the travellers, to add to the load it was intended to lighten; while I observed in others, that so cheap a kindness as a mild word, or even an affectionate look, made a poor burdened wretch move on cheerily. The bare feeling that some human being cared for him, seemed to lighten the load.

But to return to this kind neighbor. She had a little old book in her hand, the covers of which were worn out by much use. When she saw the blind woman ready to faint, she would read her a few words out of this book, such as the following: "Blessed are the poor in spirit; for theirs is the kingdom of heaven." "Blessed are they that mourn; for they shall be comforted." "I will never leave thee, nor forsake thee." "For our light affliction, which is but for a moment, worketh out for us a far more exceeding and eternal weight of glory;" and one of these little promises operated like a cordial on the sufferer.

THE CLERGYMAN.

A pious minister sinking under the weight of a distressed parish, whose worldly wants he was totally unable to bear, was suddenly relieved by a good widow, who came up, and took all the sick and hungry on her own shoulders. The burden of the parish thus divided became tolerable. The minister being no longer bowed down by the temporal distresses of his people, applied himself cheerfully to his own part of the weight. And it was pleasant to see how those two persons, neither of them very strong, or rich, or healthy, by thus kindly uniting together, were enabled to bear the weight of a whole parish; though singly, either of them must have sunk under the attempt. And I remember one great grief I felt during my whole journey was, that I did not see more of this union and concurring kindness, by which all the burdens might have been easily divided. It troubled me to observe, that of all the laws of the valley, there was not one more frequently broken than the law of kindness.

THE NEGROES.

I now spied a swarm of poor black men, women, and children, a multitude which no man could number; these groaned, and toiled, and sweated, and bled under far heavier loads than I had yet seen. But for a while no man helped them; at length a few white travellers were touched with the sorrowful sighing of those millions, and very heartily did they put their hands to the burdens; but their number was not quite equal to the work they had undertaken: I perceived, however, that they never lost sight of these poor, heavyladen wretches; and as the number of these generous helpers increased, and is continually increasing, I felt a comfortable hope, that before all the blacks got out of the valley, the whites would so apply themselves to the burden, that the loads would be effectually lightened.

Among the travellers, I had occasion to remark, that those who most kicked and struggled under their burdens, only made them so much the heavier; for their shoulders became extremely galled by these vain struggles. The load, if borne patiently, would in the end have turned even to the advantage of the bearersfor so the Lord of the valley had kindly decreed; but as to these grumblers, they had all the smart and none of the benefit. But the thing that made all these burdens seem so very heavy was, that in every one, without exception, there was a certain inner packet, which most of the travellers took pains to conceal, and carefully wrap up; and while they were forward enough to complain of the other part of their burdens, few said a word about this, though in truth it was the pressing weight of this secret packet which served to render the general burden so intolerable.

In spite of all their caution, I contrived to get a peep at it. I found, in each, that this packet had the same label: the word sin was written on all as a general title, and in ink so black that they could not wash it out. I observed that most of them took no small pains to hide the writing; but I was surprised to see that they did not try to get rid of their load, but the label. If any kind friend who assisted these people in bearing their burdens, did but so much as hint at the secret packet, or advise them to get rid of it, they took fire at once, and commonly denied that they had any such article in their portmanteau; and it was those whose secret packet swelled to the most enormous size, who most stoutly denied they had any such packet at all.

I saw with pleasure, however, that some who had long labored heartily to get rid of this inward packet, at length, by prayers, and tears, and efforts, not made in their own strength, found it much diminished, and the more this packet shrunk in size, the lighter was the other part of their burdens also.

Then, methought, all at once, I heard a voice as it had been the voice of an angel, crying out, and saying, "Ye unhappy pilgrims, why are ye troubled about the burden which ye are doomed to bear through this Valley of Tears? Know ye not, that as soon as ye shall have escaped out of this valley, the whole burden shall drop off, provided ye neglect not to remove that inward weight of sin which principally oppresses you? Study, then, the whole will of the Lord of this valley. Learn from him how the heavy part of your burdens may now be lessened, and how at last it shall be removed for ever. Be comforted. Faith and hope may cheer you even in this valley. The passage, though it seems long to weary travellers, is comparatively short; for beyond it there is a land of everlasting rest, 'where ye shall hunger no more, neither thirst any more; where ye shall be led by living fountains of waters, and all tears shall be wiped away from your eyes.'"

THE STRAIT GATE AND THE BROAD WAY:

BEING THE SECOND PART OF
THE VALLEY OF TEARS.

BY HANNAH MORE.

Now I had a second vision of what was passing in the Valley of Tears. Methought I saw again the same kind of travellers whom I had seen in the former part, and they were wandering at large through the same vast wilderness. At first setting out on his journey, each traveller had a small lamp so fixed in his bosom, that it seemed to make a part of himself; but as this natural light did not prove to be sufficient to direct them in the right way, the King of the country, in pity to their wanderings and their blindness, out of his gracious condescension, promised to give these poor wayfaring people an additional supply of light from his own royal treasury.

But as he did not choose to lavish his favors where there seemed no disposition to receive them, he would not bestow any of his oil on such as did not think it worth asking for. "Ask, and ye shall receive," was the universal rule he laid down for them. Many were prevented from asking through pride and vanity, for they thought they had light enough already; preferring the feeble glimmerings of their own lamp, to all the offered light from the King's treasury.

Yet it was observed of those who rejected it as thinking they had enough, that hardly any acted up to what even their own natural light showed them. Others were deterred from asking, because they were told that this light not only pointed out the dangers and difficulties of the road, but by a certain reflecting power it turned inward on themselves, and revealed to them ugly sights in their own hearts to which they rather chose to be blind; for those travellers "chose darkness rather than light, because their deeds were evil." Now it was remarkable that these two properties were inseparable, and that the lamp would be of little outward use, except to those who used it as an internal reflector. A threat and a promise also never failed to accompany the offer of this light from the King: a promise, that to those who improved what they had, more should be given; and a threat, that from those who did not use it wisely, should be taken away even what they had.

I observed that when the road was very dangerous, when terrors and difficulties and death beset the faithful traveller, then, on their fervent importunity, the King voluntarily gave large and bountiful supplies of light, such as in common seasons never could have been expected; always proportioning the quantity given to the necessity of the case: "As their day was," such was their light and strength.

Though many chose to depend entirely on their own lamp, yet it was observed that this light was apt to go out, if left to itself. It was easily blown out by those violent gusts which were perpetually howling through the wilderness, and indeed it was the natural tendency of that unwholesome atmosphere to extinguish it; just as you have seen a candle go out when exposed to the vapors and foul air of a damp room. It was a melancholy sight to see multitudes of travellers heedlessly pacing on, boasting they had light enough, and despising the offer of more.

But what astonished me most of all was, to see many, and some of them, too, accounted men of firstrate wit, actually busy in blowing out their own light, because, while any spark of it remained, it only served to torment them, and point out things which they did not wish to see. And having once blown out their own light, they were not easy till they had blown out that of their neighbor's also; so that a good part of the wilderness seemed to exhibit a sort of universal blindman'sbuff, each endeavoring to catch his neighbor, while his own voluntary blindness exposed him to be caught himself, so that each was actually falling into the snare he was laying for another; till at length, as selfishness is the natural consequence of blindness, "catch he that catch can," became the general cry throughout the wilderness.

Now I saw in my vision, that there were some others who were busy in strewing the most gaudy flowers over the numerous bogs, precipices, and pitfalls, with which the wilderness abounded; and thus making danger and death look so gay, that the poor thoughtless creatures seemed to delight in their own destruction. Those pitfalls did not appear deep or dangerous to the eye, because over them were raised gay edifices with alluring names. These were filled with singing men and singing women, and with dancing, and feasting, and gaming, and drinking, and jollity, and madness. But though the scenery was gay, the footing was unsound. The floors were full of holes, through which the unthinking merrymakers were continually sinking. Some tumbled through in the middle of a song, many at the end of a feast; and though there was many a cup of intoxication wreathed with flowers, yet there was always poison at the bottom.

But what most surprised me was, that though no day passed over their heads in which some of these merrymakers did not drop through, yet their loss made little impression on those who were left. Nay, instead of being awakened to more circumspection and selfdenial by the continual dropping off of those about them, several of them seemed to borrow from thence an argument of a directly contrary tendency, and the very shortness of the time was only urged as a reason to use it more sedulously for the indulgence of sensual delights. "Let us eat and drink; for tomorrow we die." "Let us crown ourselves with rosebuds before they are withered." With these, and a thousand other such little mottoes, the gay garlands of the wilderness were decorated.

Some admired poets were set to work to set the most corrupt sentiments to the most harmonious tunes: these were sung without scruple, chiefly, indeed, by the looser sons of riot, but not seldom also by the more orderly daughters of sobriety, who were not ashamed to sing, to the sound of instruments, sentiments so corrupt and immoral, that they would have blushed to speak or read them; but the music seemed to sanctify the corruption, especially such as was connected with love or drinking.

Now I observed, that all the travellers who had so much as a spark of life left, seemed every now and then, as they moved onwards, to cast an eye, though with very different degrees of attention, towards the Happy land, which they were told lay at the end of their journey; but as they could not see very far forward, and as they knew there was a dark and shadowy valley, which must needs be crossed before they could attain to the Happy land, they tried to turn their attention from it as much as they could. The truth is, they were not sufficiently apt to consult a map which the King had given them, and which pointed out the road to the Happy land so clearly, that the "wayfaring man, though simple, could not err." This map also defined very correctly the boundaries of the Happy land from the land of Misery, both of which lay on the other side of the dark and shadowy valley; but so many beacons and lighthouses were erected, so many clear and explicit directions furnished for avoiding the one country and attaining the other, that it was not the King's fault, if even one single traveller got wrong. But I am inclined to think, that in spite of the map, and the King's word, and his offers of assistance to get them thither, the travellers in general did not heartily and truly believe, after all, that there was any such country as the Happy land; or at least, the paltry and transient pleasures of the wilderness so besotted them, the thoughts of the dark and shadowy valley so frightened them, that they thought they should be more comfortable by banishing all thought and forecast.

Now I also saw in my dream, that there were two roads through the wilderness, one of which every traveller must needs take. The first was narrow, and difficult, and rough, but it was infallibly safe. It did not admit the traveller to stray either to the right hand or to the left, yet it was far from being destitute of real comforts or sober pleasures. The other was a broad and tempting way, abounding with luxurious fruits and gaudy flowers to tempt the eye and please the appetite. To forget the dark valley, through which every traveller was well assured he must one day pass, seemed, indeed, the object of general desire. To this great end, all that human ingenuity could invent was industriously set to work. The travellers read, and they wrote, and they painted, and they sung, and they danced, and they drank as they went along, not so much because they all cared for these things, or had any real joy in them, as because this restless activity served to divert their attention from ever being fixed on the dark and shadowy valley.

The King, who knew the thoughtless temper of the travellers, and how apt they were to forget their journey's end, had thought of a thousand little kind attentions to warn them of their dangers. And as we sometimes see in our gardens written on a board in great letters, "Beware of springguns""Mantraps are set here;" so had this King caused to be written and stuck up, before the eyes of the travellers, several little notices and cautions, such as, "Broad is the way that leadeth to destruction;" "Take heed, lest ye also perish;" "Woe to them that rise up early to drink wine;" "The pleasures of sin are but for a season."

Such were the notices directed to the Broadway travellers; but they were so busily engaged in plucking the flowers, sometimes before they were blown, and in devouring the fruits, often before they were ripe, and in loading themselves with yellow clay, under the weight of which millions perished, that they had no time so much as to look at the King's directions.

Many went wrong because they preferred a merry journey to a safe one, and because they were terrified by certain notices chiefly intended for the Narrowway travellers, such as, "Ye shall weep and lament, but the world shall rejoice;" but had these foolish people allowed themselves time or patience to read to the end, which they seldom would do, they would have seen these comfortable words added: "But your sorrow shall be turned into joy;" also, "Your joy no man taketh from you;" and, "They that sow in tears shall reap in joy."

Now I also saw in my dream, that many travellers who had a strong dread of ending at the land of Misery, walked up to the Strait gate, hoping, that though the entrance was narrow, yet if they could once get in, the road would widen; but what was their grief, when on looking more closely they saw written on the inside, "Narrow is the way:" this made them take fright; they compared the inscriptions with which the whole way was lined, such as, "Be ye not conformed to this world""Deny yourselves, take up your cross," with all the tempting pleasures of the wilderness.

Some indeed recollected the fine descriptions they had read of the Happy land, the Golden city, and the river of Pleasures, and they sighed; but then, those joys were distant, and from the faintness of their light they soon got to think that what was remote might be uncertain; and while the present good increased in bulk by its nearness, the distant good receded, diminished, disappeared. Their faith failed; they would trust no farther than they could see: they drew back and got into the Broadway, taking a common but sad refuge in the number and gayety of their companions.

When these fainthearted people, who yet had set out well, turned back, their light was quite put out, and then they became worse than those who had made no attempt to get in; "for it is impossible," that is, it is next to impossible, "for those who were once enlightened, and have tasted of the heavenly gift, and the good word of God, and the powers of the world to come, if they shall fall away, to renew them again to repentance."

A few honest, humble travellers, not naturally stronger than the rest, but strengthened by their trust in the King's word, came up by the light of their lamps, and meekly entered in at the Strait gate. As they advanced farther they felt less heavy, and though the way did not in reality grow wider, yet they grew reconciled to the narrowness of it, especially when they saw the walls here and there studded with certain jewels called promises, such as, "He that endureth to the end shall be saved;" and, "My grace is sufficient for thee."

Some, when they were almost ready to faint, were encouraged by seeing that many niches in the Narrowway were filled with statues and pictures of saints and martyrs, who had borne their testimony at the stake, that the Narrowway was the safe way; and these travellers, instead of sinking at the sight of the painted wheel and gibbet, the sword and the furnace, were animated by these words written under them: "Those that wear white robes came out of great tribulation;" and, "Be ye followers of them who through faith and patience inherit the promises."

In the meantime there came a great multitude of travellers, all from Laodicea: this was the largest party I had yet seen; these were neither cold nor hot; they would not give up future hope, they could not endure present pain; so they contrived to deceive themselves by fancying, that though they resolved to keep the Happy land in view, yet there must needs be many different ways which led to it, no doubt all equally sure without being all equally rough; so they set on foot certain little contrivances to attain the end without using the means, and softened down the spirit of the King's directions to fit them to their own practice.

Sometimes they would split a direction in two, and only use that half which suited them. For instance, when they met with the following rule, "Trust in the Lord, and do good," they would take the first half, and make themselves easy with a general sort of trust, that through the mercy of the King all would go well with them, though they themselves did nothing. And on the other hand, many made sure that a few good works of their own would carry them safely to the Happy land, though they did not trust in the Lord, nor place any faith in his word: so they took the second half of the spliced direction. Thus some perished by a lazy faith, and others by a working pride.

A large party of Pharisees now appeared, who had so neglected their lamp that they did not see their way at all, though they fancied themselves to be full of light; they kept up appearances so well as to delude others, and most effectually to delude themselves with a notion that they might be found in the right way at last. In this dreadful delusion they went on to the end, and till they were finally plunged in the dark valley, never discovered the horrors which awaited them on the dismal shore. It was remarkable, that while these Pharisees were often boasting how bright their light burned, in order to get the praise of men, the humble travellers, whose steady light showed their good works to others, refused all commendation, and the brighter their light shined before men, so much the more they insisted that they ought to glory, not in themselves, but their Father which is in heaven.

I now set myself to observe what was the particular let, molestation, and hinderance, which obstructed particular travellers in their endeavors to enter in at the Strait gate. I remarked a huge portly man, who seemed desirous of getting in, but he carried about him such a vast provision of bags full of gold, and had on so many rich garments which stuffed him out so wide, that though he pushed and squeezed like one who had really a mind to get in, yet he could not possibly do so. Then I heard a voice crying, "Woe to him that loadeth himself with thick clay." The poor man felt something was wrong, and even went so far as to change some of his more cumbersome vanities into others which seemed less bulky; but still he and his pack were much too wide for the gate.

He would not, however, give up the matter so easily, but began to throw away a little of the coarser part of his baggage; but still I remarked, that he threw away none of the vanities which lay near his heart. He tried again, but it would not do; still his dimensions were too large. He now looked up and read these words: "How hardly shall they who have riches enter into the kingdom of God!" The poor man sighed to find that it was impossible to enjoy his fill of both worlds, and "went away sorrowing." If he ever afterwards cast a thought towards the Happy land, it was only to regret that the road which led to it was too narrow to admit any but the meagre children of want, who were not so encumbered by wealth as to be too big for the passage. Had he read on, he would have seen that "with God all things are possible."

Another advanced with much confidence of success; for having little worldly riches or honors, the gate did not seem so strait to him. He got to the threshold triumphantly, and seemed to look back with disdain on all that he was quitting. He soon found, however, that he was so bloated with pride, and stuffed out with selfsufficiency, that he could not get in. Nay, he was in a worse way than the rich man just named, for he was willing to throw away some of his outward luggage; whereas this man refused to part with a grain of that vanity and selfapplause which made him too big for the way. The sense of his own worth so swelled him out, that he stuck fast in the gateway, and could neither get in nor out.

Finding now that he must cut off all those big thoughts of himself, if he wished to be reduced to such a size as to pass the gate, he gave up all thoughts of it. He scorned that humility and selfdenial which might have shrunk him down to the proper dimensions: the more he insisted on his own qualifications for entrance, the more impossible it became to enter, for the bigger he grew. Finding that he must become quite another manner of man before he could hope to get in, he gave up the desire; and I now saw, that though when he set his face towards the Happy land he could not get an inch forward, yet the instant he made a motion to turn back into the world, his speed became rapid enough, and he got back into the Broadway much sooner than he had got out of it.

Many, who for a time were brought down from their usual bulk by some affliction, seemed to get in with ease. They now thought all their difficulties over; for having been surfeited with the world during their late disappointment, they turned their backs upon it willingly enough. A fit of sickness perhaps, which is very apt to reduce, had for a time brought their bodies into subjection, so that they were enabled just to get in at the gateway; but as soon as health and spirits returned, the way grew narrower and narrower to them; they could not get on, but turned short, and got back into the world.

I saw many attempt to enter who were stopped short by a large burden of worldly cares; others by a load of idolatrous attachments; but I observed that nothing proved a more complete bar than that vast bundle of prejudices with which multitudes were loaded. Others were fatally obstructed by loads of bad habits which they would not lay down, though they knew they prevented their entrance. Some few, however, of most descriptions who had kept their light alive by craving constant supplies from the King's treasury, got through at last by a strength which they felt not to be their own.

One poor man, who carried the largest bundle of bad habits I had seen, could not get on a step; he never ceased, however, to implore for light enough to see where his misery lay: he threw down one of his bundles, then another, but all to little purpose, still he could not stir. At last, striving as if in agonywhich is the true way of enteringhe threw down the heaviest article in his pack: this was selfishness. The poor fellow felt relieved at once, his light burned brightly, and the rest of his pack was as nothing.

Then I heard a great noise as of carpenters at work. I looked to see what this might be, and saw many sturdy travellers, who, finding they were too bulky to get through, took into their heads not to reduce themselves, but to widen the gate: they hacked on this side, and hewed on that; but all their hacking and hewing and hammering was to no purpose, they got only their labor for their pains: it would have been possible for them to have reduced themselves, but to widen the Narrowway was impossible.

What grieved me most was, to observe that many who had got on successfully a good way, now stopped to rest, and to admire their own progress. While they were thus valuing themselves on their attainment, their light diminished. While these were boasting how far they had left others behind, who had set out much earlier, some slower travellers, whose beginning had not been so promising but who had walked circumspectly, now outstripped them. These last walked, "not as though they had already attained," but "this one thing they did, forgetting the things which were behind, they pressed forward towards the mark for the prize of their high calling." These, though naturally weak, yet by "laying aside every weight, finished the race that was before them."

Those who had kept their "light burning," who were not "wise in their own conceit," who "laid their help on One that is mighty," who had "chosen to suffer affliction rather than to enjoy the pleasures of sin for a season," came at length to the Happy land. They had indeed the dark and shadowy valley to cross; but even there they found "a rod and a staff" to comfort them. Their light, instead of being put out by the damps of the valley of the Shadow of Death, often burned with added brightness.

Some, indeed, suffered the terrors of a short eclipse; but even then their light, like that of a dark lantern, was not put out, it was only hid for a while; and even these often finished their course with joy. But be that as it might, the instant they reached the Happy land, all tears were wiped from their eyes; and the King himself came forth and welcomed them into his presence, and put a crown upon their heads, with these words: "Well done, good and faithful servant; enter thou into the joy of thy LORD."

I mean here, however, to accommodate the parable to the purpose of showing in what manner the gospel often addresses itself to men in different periods of life, calling one at an early age, and one much later, into the same vineyard of Christ. We are in no danger of erring exactly as the Jews did, by raising objections to Christ's calling the great body of the Gentile nations into his church. We may be in great danger, however, of acting much in the same spirit with the Jews, and if we do so, that spirit is most likely to show itself in our objecting to extend the privileges of the gospel to some poor outcasts or aged sinners among ourselves.

First, then, I will put the case of one who is brought to obey the gospel in the morning of life, and is one of the youngest of the laborers in our Lord's vineyard. He sets out well, as I will suppose, and goes on well through all the following stages of life; even his most early prayers are not a mere matter of form, but they spring out of a persuasion already rising up in his mind, that he is entirely dependent on God, and needs the help of his Holy Spirit. It pleases God, in answer to his infant prayers, to strengthen this child against his early temptations, so that he does as Christ commands, and not as wicked children may require or expect of him. Such a child as this will also be diligent in learning his lessons, and improving his time; for he will be like the laboring men in the vineyard, spoken of in the parable, and not like the idle ones in the marketplace.

Now what a vast quantity of good may such a person be the means of doing in the course of a long life on earth. First of all, he is a blessing to his young connections and schoolfellows, for he will often reprove vice and irreligion in them, even though it should be much against the modesty of his own natural inclinations. Then he grows up to be a bold witness for God in the face of all the gay and unthinking young men or women among whom he is thrown in early life. Next, he proceeds to do good about the village or town where he is settled. After this, perhaps, he marries, when his wife, and all her connections, and his own offspring also, have the advantage of observing him. They remark his humble, candid, pious, and affectionate spirit, and his diligent and selfdenying life, and they profit both by his kind services and his example.

Now, too, his income very probably increases through his good character and industry, and hence he is able to assist the poor, the fatherless, the widow, and to pay for the instruction of the ignorant; for he spends little on himself. Having no vices he has few wants, and his family, being trained to religious habits, and preserved from the gay and expensive customs of the world, have few wants also. Thus is happiness of all kinds spread abroad. He explains, also, as he has opportunity, those Christian doctrines which have led him into this life of usefulness, and is a great promoter of the gospel, so that a little world of Christians is continually gathering together around him, and even a new generation is coming forward, which shall, by and by, rise up and call him blessed.

THE PARABLE OF THE LABORERS
IN THE VINEYARD.

The kingdom of heaven is compared by our Saviour to "a householder which went out early in the morning to hire laborers into his vineyard. And again he went out about the third hour, and saw others standing idle in the marketplace, and said unto them, Go ye also into the vineyard: and they went their way. And he went out about the sixth and ninth hour, and did likewise. And about the eleventh hour he went out, and found others standing idle, and saith unto them, Why stand ye here all the day idle? They say unto him, Because no man hath hired us. He saith unto them, Go ye also into the vineyard; and whatsoever is right, that shall ye receive."

By the householder here spoken of, our Saviour himself is intended; and by the laborers hired into the vineyard, those persons are meant who enter into his service. These laborers are said to be found standing idle in the marketplace; for the gospel finds men idle, that is, not employed in God's service. They are working busily enough, perhaps, for themselves; for men will rise up early, and go to bed late, for the sake of getting money, or following pleasure; but then their diligence is of a wrong kind. They are not diligent in the way of duty to their Maker. They may be likened to a certain kind of servants, who though they may seem busy, and may get from ignorant persons some credit for being so, are nevertheless merely running on their own errands, and doing their own work, so that they are no better than idle in respect to the work which they ought to be doing for their householder or master.

But when they become true Christians they are no longer like those idle fellows who are always sauntering about with their arms folded, in the marketplace, pretending that they are in want of employment, no man having as yet hired them: they may now be compared to a set of laborers in the vineyard or garden, who, whenever you look at them, are sure to be seen either digging, or planting, or watering, or doing, in short, whatever is most wanting in the place where they are working; and they have always an eye, moreover, to the honor and interests of the great Householder their Master.

The householder is said to go out at different hours of the day to hire these servants. This signifies that the light of revelation was sent at different periods of the world to the different people in it, and in particular to the Jews at one period, and the Gentile nations at another. The Jews had been much offended at seeing Christ address himself to the Gentiles, who, as they thought, not having been called into the church or vineyard of God at an early period of the world, ought not to be received at a later hour. Our Saviour, therefore, makes use of this parable, or story, as a convenient means of showing how unreasonable these Jewish prejudices were.

In the midst of all this usefulness, however, he is very modest and lowly. He gives God the praise of every good thing he does, and he is sincerely pained when flattering and inconsiderate people load him with their extravagant commendations; for he sees a thousand faults in himself which he is much engaged in overcoming, though others perceive them not. He is conscious of neglecting many an opportunity of doing good, and of failing to suppress sufficiently many an evil thought; and though some irreligious people may fancy that he already carries things too far, as they absurdly term it, yet there is nothing of which he is himself more sure than that he falls short in every duty, and especially in those things of which they least see the importancesin zeal for religion, in the duties of prayer and praise, and in all the feelings and expressions of gratitude to his Creator and Redeemer.

But while we are thus describing the amiable character of a Christian, let it be remarked also, that he meets with various difficulties, and is exposed to not a few misrepresentations, His virtuous singularity, for instance, is considered by some, who do not understand his principles, to be unnecessary preciseness, and is thought to arise from a conceited or disobliging spirit. His courage in reproving vice, if unsuccessful, is called, by those whom he reproves, impertinence. His activity in doing good is not seldom ascribed to forwardness. Even his extraordinary liberality is accounted for, by those who do not care to follow his example, by saying that it is mere vanity, or lavish imprudence. And, above all, his piety is apt to be thought, by the impious and irreligious, to be mere hypocrisy, or at best a poor, pitiable sort of weakness.

Thus, then, while the Christian has many peculiar hopes, and joys, and consolations on the one hand, he experiences many trials and hardships on the other. Nevertheless, he bears up under them all; many of them, indeed, appear light to him in comparison of what they seem to other men, and grow more and more light as he becomes used to them. He goes on, therefore, cheerful and contented: he labors much, he suffers much, he renounces much, he contends much in the cause of Christ; and he does this in every place to which he moves, in every changing situation and circumstance, and in every season of life through which he passes.

And now at last, after a long life, death closes in upon him; he looks with thankfulness back to what is past, and with composure to the important and decisive hour that is approaching. He trusts, indeed, not in himself, but in his Saviour, for, after all, he is but "an unprofitable servant, having done no more than it was his duty to do;" but he has much comfortable proof that his Christian faith has not been a mere name; and he is able to take up the same language with the apostle, and to say, with a measure of the same confidence, "I have fought a good fight, I have finished my course, I have kept the faith; henceforth there is laid up for me a crown of righteousness, which the Lord the righteous Judge shall give me at that day." This then is one of those who, to borrow the phrase in the parable, may be said to have "borne the burden and heat of the day."

There is another class of persons who may now be spoken of as entering into the vineyard of Christ at a somewhat later hour; at the age, we will suppose, of twentyfive or thirty. These have lost an hour indeed; they have idled away one precious season of life. Alas, it is also to be feared, that during the heat and selfconfidence of youth, they have done much evil, as well as neglected to do good. Perhaps it has also happened that they have already formed some rash connection, and established themselves on some irreligious plan; but now they repent; they break through all difficulties; they turn away from the path in which they had set out in life, and they turn into the vineyard of Christ. They become humble, diligent, and useful Christians; for even those also give a good part at least of their health and strength to the cause of their Saviour, and with grief and shame at having been thus far idle, they become fellowlaborers with those happier persons already spoken of.

But let us come to a class of persons who repent somewhat later still; I mean at the age of forty or fifty. How affecting is the condition of such persons when it is well considered. They now discover that they have been all their lives living, as it were, to no purpose; that the whole of these forty or fifty years has been idly thrown away, or if spent in labor, it has been mere labor in vain. For even though they may have been diligent, yet they have been merely diligent in doing their own will, and not the will of God; they have been working in their own vineyard, and not in the vineyard of Christ; they have been year after year pushing their own fortune, building up their own credit, exalting their own consequence, indulging their own ease, following their own pleasure, caring about their own interest, or family interest, while the great interests of the kingdom of Christ have been quite out of the question.

Now, therefore, they have to repent perhaps of the very things they have been the most proud of. They have also to resist many sinful habits which have become, as it were, a second nature; they have to disentangle themselves from a multitude of irreligious connections, whose opinions have hitherto ruled over them; they have to unteach even their own children many a false principle which they had taught them. With many a weary and painful step, they have to measure back the whole ground which they have been treading; and they have to undo, as it were, every thing which for fifty years they have been doing. When more than half of life is over, they have to enter upon the work which they were sent into the world to do; but at length they hire themselves into the vineyard of Christ, and he receives them, though it is the ninth hour: and now they husband well their time, and begin to be fruitful in every good work; and whatever they do, they do all to the glory of God: they perform what he commands, and simply because he commands it: they become a part of the church of Christ, and are numbered among the laborers in his vineyard.

But if the case of such as were last spoken of is affecting, what shall be said of those aged persons whom it still remains for us to describe? Some there arebut, alas, it is to be feared, that it is the case of very fewwho even at seventy, or more than seventy years old, repent, and become the servants of Christ When scarcely an hour of life remains, when the evening is closing in, and the "night cometh in which no man can work," then it pleases God to send his grace possibly to a few of these also, and they go for the short hour that remains into the same vineyard of Christ.

How mournful is the view which we have now to take of such an aged sinner's condition. Here is a person, the whole term of whose earthly existence, one poor uncertain hour excepted, has been spent in a sinful course. How plain is it in his case, that there can be no such thing as merit, and that if ever he is saved, it must be through the mere mercy of Goda doctrine, indeed, which is equally true in the case of all. Let us run over the woful tale of his wicked life, and as before we thought fit to describe an eminent and distinguished Christian, so now, by way of making the difference more particularly striking, let us draw the picture of one who, though no thief or murderer, and therefore not accounted one of the most abandoned of mankind, yet is lying under a load of much more than ordinary guilt. Those persons who feel themselves guilty of any part of the crimes we shall enumerate, should take their share of the reproof, and if they have not repented, so as to enter into the vineyard of Christ, they should remember, that though they may be criminals of a smaller size, yet they are still remaining under condemnation.

To a perverse and disobedient childhood has succeeded, as we will suppose, a wild and vicious youth, and then a proud and ambitious manhood, and after this a fretful or covetous old age. In the course of his long life many temptations have broken in upon him, and by turns he has yielded to them all. Many different situations have been filled by him, and in each, as he now sees, he has either neglected or betrayed his trust. He has been a negligent and bad father, an unreasonable, nay, secretly an unfaithful husband, a careless inattentive brother, a hollow, flattering, and designing friend; perhaps, also, a mean timeserving politician, and even a mischievous common acquaintance. Do you ask what has been the turn of his common conversation? Instead of being pious, useful, benevolent, candid, and sincere, it has at one time been proud and passionate, at another vain and flourishing, at another slanderous and revengeful; now again, it has been selfish, crafty, and dissembling, often also daringly impious and profane, and not seldom exceedingly polluting and impure. Do you ask what have been the sinful deeds he has done? O what a dreadful variety has there been in them! At one time he has been trying to overreach his fellowtrader; at another, he has been endeavoring to seduce some unhappy maiden: at one time he is seen quarrelling with his neighbor; at another, he falls out with one of his own family, after which he grows mad with every one around him, and, at last, equally mad and out of humor with himself. He has been selfish, griping, and avaricious on all occasions, and what he has saved or gained by oppression and fraud, he has spent on his profligacy: he has got drunk with the money which he has acquired by dishonesty, and he has paid for his debauchery at night by the sum which he has contrived in the morning to keep back from the poor. At the same time he has been turbulent, factious, and complainingalways talking of what is amiss in others, and very sudden and severe in judging them, but very proud and confident in himself, disdaining even the smallest blame. Would you get into favor with him, you must flatter him at every word; and you will please him best by doing it grossly and to his face, for he is quite used to praise: he has long lived among those who look up to him as their patron, or gape at him as their principal wit, or glory in him as their chief songster, possibly as the chairman of their drinking club, and as their merry leader in debauchery.

To all these sins he adds that of being the decided enemy of every religious man. Is the gospel preached at his very door, he stands in the front rank of its enemies; he denies its efficacy, makes a joke of its doctrines, reviles its followers, and is the avowed hinderer of its progress. Christianity, indeed, is against him, and therefore it is no wonder that he is against Christianity. Hence it is, that the religion of every man around him, however pure and excellent, if it is but zealous and fervent, is declared, without distinction, to be mere hypocrisy, enthusiasm, bigotry, and cant.

But let us look a little also to the various consequences of his life of sin. Who can trace a thousandth part of the miseries which have arisen even from one single source; I mean from the levity and inconsideration which have made one leading feature in his character? Who can calculate the effects of all those evil principles which he has scattered at random, reaching even to distant places and generations? Who can calculate the mischief which he may have caused even in one of his light convivial hours? View the inscription on that gravestone, which is now almost overgrown with thorns. Ah, it is the name of an old companion, an alehouse friend, who once used to sing with him, in one joyful chorus, "the praises of the flowing bowl," and who thus was encouraged in those habits of intemperance which led to that untimely grave.

Let us open one other source of no less painful reflection. Behold that miserable female, once the gay partner of his guilty pleasures, whom if he has not been the first to seduce, he has at least carried on and confirmed in a life of sin, and whom he has left afterwards to sink in want, to grow loathsome through disease, and to become a nuisance to the village or the town. He has helped to ruin but not to deliver her; he has soon left her to the tender mercies of some of her own sex as hardened as herself, among whom she has sunk, and groaned, and died.

Which way, then, shall this aged sinner turn his eyes? Every scene, every place, every month and day of his life, which he can call to remembrance, reminds him of some sin. Shall he look to some of his more reputable actions? Alas, even when his conduct has been most creditable, his motives have been unchristian and impure. "True, I have had some character," he now says to himself, "but I have had no title to it. Men have not known me; or if a few have known me, and yet praised me, they have praised me because they have wanted to carry some point of their own by pleasing me: nay, my companions have even praised me for what was evil, for the same people seem now, methinks, to blame me in proportion as they discern any thing in me that is good." Thus the recollection of the applauses he used to receive from these wicked men is one aggravation of his pain.

But shall he look to his more innocent and early years? Alas, the review of his infancy only serves to remind him how naturally and how soon he went astray; how soon "he forsook the guide of his youth, and forgot the covenant of his God." Thus, if he looks backward, all is misery, and horror, and despair. Shall he then look forward and comfort himself by thinking how effectually he will repair all the evil he has done? But how shall he now repair it? Of those whom he has corrupted many are dead, and of the survivors very few can now be found. Go, then, and bring these few back to God. Alas, one will mock, another will dissemble, a third will despise. Go, try to reclaim even the children of thine own loins, who are all trained through thy means in an evil course. Nay, even these also will scoff at thy rebuke, and say, "Our old father is grown troublesome and peevish through age; he is turned religious only because he has just done with this life, and has one foot in the grave."

What then, I say, can this aged sinner do to remedy the evils he has caused? He can only abhor himself for what is past, and repent sincerely of all that he has done. See him then at length abhorring himself, and "repenting in dust and ashes." See him retiring to his chamber, and, for the first time, communing seriously with his own heart. See him reviewing the whole of his past life, from the first dawn of reason to the present hour, endeavoring to survey with exactness his thoughts, words, and actions, and all his most secret practices, intentions, and inclinations. See him meditating also on his numberless omissions, taking the law of God for his rule, and beginning now, for the first time, to discover what manner of person he has been. How does he stand amazed at his own former stupidity and blindness and hardness of heart, and how astonished also at the patience of God, which has so long borne with him.

And now his heart relents, the tears of penitential sorrow begin to flow; the lion also is changed into a lamb, and the same person who before might have been compared to the woman in the gospel, "out of whom there went seven devils," or to "Saul breathing out threatenings and slaughter," may now be likened to the Magdalen weeping at the feet of Jesus, or to Paul trembling and astonished, and crying out, as he lay on the ground, "Lord, what wilt thou have me to do?" or to the same Paul, when it was afterwards said of him, "Behold, he prayeth." With trembling limbs, and with a body bowed down with age, behold then this repenting sinner walking to that public worship which he had so long neglected; with weak and failing eyes he opens the scripture; at the age of seventy he begins to inquire with childlike simplicity into the nature of the gospel, and knowing how short his time is, he makes haste to obey it.

And now, perhaps his old companions deride him; for as he once sneered at others who were religious, and called them all hypocrites, so is he now sneered at, and called a hypocrite in his turn: he becomes the scoff of the drunkard and the merry jest of the profane, and they that "sit in the gate make songs of him." Now also the very sins of his youth, which had been scarcely mentioned before, are brought forward by his former favorites and friends as present evidence against him; his crimes are even aggravated, and are all blazed abroad; but it is one proof of his sincerity, that even these cutting reproaches do not shake him from his purpose, nor induce him to turn back to his old companions. No, they may laugh, they may smile at what they call his pretended sanctity, but in truth he is no hypocrite.

"The tear
That drops upon his Bible is sincere."
He is disposed to doubt, indeed, for a time, his own sincerity; for his guilt is so great, and the blessings of the gospel, including as they do the gift of eternal life, appear so large in his eyes, that he cannot at once raise his hopes so high. His sincerity is proved, however, by his proceeding to repair, as far as he has opportunity, each evil that he has done; by his mourning over what he cannot cure, and by the determination of his mind, through the help of divine grace, to walk for the future in newness of life. In short, he feels that if his life were prolonged a thousand years, and youth and health were restored to him, he should choose to spend his strength and the utmost length of his days in the service of the same Master, and to be a laborer in the same vineyard.

But here, methinks, some objector rises up, and says, "What then, shall this man be accepted of God, like him who has been moral and orderly all his days, or like the first person you mentioned?" We shall now answer this objection by proceeding with the parable.

The Jews are there represented as murmuring against the good man of the house, on account of his rewarding the more late and early laborers, the ancient Jews and the newly converted Gentiles, by giving each of them a penny, "saying, These last have wrought but one hour, and thou hast made them equal unto us, who have borne the burden and heat of the day. But he answered one of them, and said, Friend, I do thee no wrong: didst not thou agree with me for a penny? Take that thine is, and go thy way: I will give unto this last even as unto thee. Is it not lawful for me to do what I will with mine own?" It was no injury to the Jews that the poor Gentiles were admitted, though at a later hour, into the church, and the Jews had therefore no right to complain; on the contrary, they ought to have rejoiced at it. In like manner, it can be no injury to those among us who may have served Christ from our youth, that any poor outcast should be admitted to the same Christian privileges with ourselves; and we also ought to rejoice, as the angels of God are said to do, over one sinner that repenteth. Again it may be remarked, that even the first calling of the Jews arose not from any superior merit in them, but from the sovereign goodness of God. Surely, therefore, it was most unreasonable in those people to complain of God's extending the same mercy to the Gentiles. Much in the same manner, it may be remarked in respect to the present day, that the salvation even of the best of men arises not from any merit of their own, but merely from God's free mercy in Christ; and surely, therefore, one pardoned sinner among us ought not to complain of the extension of the same pardon to another.

But the parable, in the two last verses of it, proceeds a step further, for it is there added by our Saviour, "Is thine eye evil because I am good?" which is as if he said, "What, do you take offence then at my being so merciful? Does it provoke your envy to see a vile Gentile called at the eleventh hour, and made equal to yourselves, who profess to have been the people of God from the beginning, and to have borne the whole burden and heat of the day?" Some very awful words are then added, wherein it is implied, that they who are ready to make this objection, brought thereby their own religious character into suspicion; and that these very penitents of the eleventh hour, whom they now presumed to despise, should hereafter even take place above themfor it is said, "So the first shall be last, and the last first; for many are called, but few chosen."

These words appear to be a prophecy of our Judge, which relates to the great day of judgment. Then many a popular but irreligious character, many a one who has been praised to the stars in this ignorant and misjudging world, and whose supposed virtues have both deceived himself, and dazzled all around him, shall sink at once into everlasting shame and disgrace; while many a poor, despised, yet repenting sinner, shall come forward and receive his crown of glory.

O, what a wonderful change in many of the appearances which we now see, shall we witness on the day of judgment. Let us not fail to remark, that then also many a false though flaming professor of the gospel, many a vain, forward, and conceited teacher, many a selfconfident enthusiast, and many a narrowminded and fiery bigot, who has spent his life in little else than in judging and condemning others, shall be brought forward in the face of the assembled world, and shall receive his own condemnation.

Then also many a diffident and trembling believer, and many a meek and lowly Christian, who has been laboring with little noise in some obscure corner of his Lord's vineyard, and on whom the bigots, not seeing him among their party, have presumptuously dealt damnation, shall take that prize which has been denied to those who set themselves up as judges over him, and shall be bid to enter into the joy of his Lord. "So the first shall be last, and the last first; for many are called, but few chosen."

Milton Keynes UK
Ingram Content Group UK Ltd.
UKHW050805150124
436059UK00014B/610